Storm-Wraith

Dark City

Legends of the wraiths Book 1

By

IJ Benneyworth

SCRIBE TRIBE READERS CLUB
DOWNLOAD OFFER

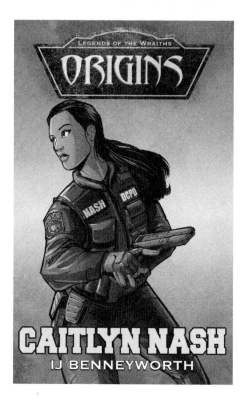

ALSO BY IJ BENNEYWORTH

Queens of the Steal

The Name of the Game

Sisterhood

The Amanda Northstar Mysteries

Dark River

Heads Will Roll

Find IJ Benneyworth at:

Web: www.scribecorps.com

Facebook: ScribeCorps

Twitter: @scribecorps

Find Doug Hills at:

Web: dnhills.com

PROLOGUE

*The capital of the Everlight Imperium goes by many names.
Officially it is Dominion City, a legacy of the country's
expansionist history in past centuries. Now the centre of a
democracy, many imperial citizens call it The Big D, for it is still
the richest and most powerful city in the land, the seat of
government and home to the Royal Family. However, those who
dwell within its walls know it by a third name, the one used most
often; Dark City.*

*For the elite, who reside in their penthouses at the top of
towering skyscrapers, the sun is never far from their skin. It is
ideal for the devout, who worship Holy Sol in private solar temples,
reciting their prayers several times between dawn and dusk. As for
the rest of the citizens, they rely on the temples at ground-level,
built to catch the sun when the angle is just right to shine through
gaps in the skyscrapers and down vast urban canyons.*

*As new towers of glass, concrete, and steel have risen, blocking
the rays and leaving many temples in the dark, so too has faith in
Sol's light dwindled. Some seek the sun wherever they can. Others*

turn to extremism and embrace the creed of flame, reckoning that holy fire generates heat and light enough while purifying the world of unbelievers. A minority turn away entirely and convert, joining the small band of moon-worshipers at the Church of Luna, an import from the sun-starved mountains and forests of Sybernia to the world's high north.

Most people, however, slide into agnosticism and atheism, fuelling a quiet despair they do not know how to overcome. The best that modern technology has to offer has improved their lives immeasurably, from the internet and smartphones to commercial flights and limitless trade from around the world. Yet, there remains an emptiness in their lives, a void where hope should be. It is unfulfilled desire for a better world unable to be born while the criminal and the corrupt press down with their iron fists. That, too, is the reason they call it Dark City, for they know it will never change and for too many the sun will never shine.

Michael Ryan hit the ground and rolled. The perimeter wall of the estate was fifteen feet high, but a large patch of dead leaves cushioned his fall. His natural athleticism took care of the rest. Michael had landed far harder and from greater heights, and collected enough scars and fractures over the years to prove it. Parkour was not the safest pass time in the slums of North Flats, universally known as the Gauntlet, but nothing was in that place. It had often been Michael's only means of a swift escape after pickpocketing or stealing larger prizes. He was left untroubled by such actions. If anyone in the slums owned something worth stealing, it was probably because they had stolen it themselves or purchased it through the exploitation of others. A pocket watch here, or an apple there; they all achieved the same goal of making it through another day.

Surviving alone for almost four years meant that Michael's conscience was severely eroded. Still, he made sure never to steal from those at the same level as him or more unfortunate, not that there were many of them. His mother, before she disappeared, had instilled in Michael the belief that even in the darkest of places, there was a glimmer of light, that there was good in the world, and if you couldn't find it, then you should be it. He had tried to cling onto that philosophy for as long as he could until the numerous beatings from youth gangs and adult abusers finally pummelled the naïvety out of him. The prospect of starvation did the rest.

Fed up of sleeping next to a different heating vent every night and conscious he was starting to be noticed a little too often, Michael ultimately decided to venture out from the Gauntlet. It had been his home for as long as he could remember, but he felt no love for it. The only place he retained any affection for was the tiny apartment he had shared with his mother. She was his only family, his father unknown. His earliest memories as a toddler were of them continuously on the move. There were flashes of vast greenery, of forests, which he supposed meant they had left Dominion City at some point. Perhaps they were dreams, though, illusions of memories never experienced. His mother tried to brighten his life as best she could. It had mainly been with love and kindness, then by expanding his mind and encouraging his imagination by reading aloud tales of chivalrous knights and placing posters of beautiful landscapes on the wall. They were poor years but happy ones.

One evening she had come back home, clearly worried, despite trying to hide it from a perceptive Michael. She asked him to fill his small backpack with the things he thought most precious but to do it quickly, for they would be leaving that night. Despite his protestations, she offered no explanation, only that she needed to head out briefly to take care of something. She kissed him goodbye before she left and promised it would take no more than an hour. That hour had lasted four years and counting.

With the rent unpaid, Michael was cast out onto the street, their possessions sold off by the landlord to line his pockets. All he had in the world was his backpack, a small cuddly lion gifted to him in the crib, and several carefully folded landscape posters. He would occasionally hug the former and stare dreamily at the latter, both reminding him of his mother. Michael sometimes wondered if she deliberately abandoned him or if something had happened to her. Was she alive or dead? The uncertainly could be crippling, so gradually, he forced the trauma to the back of his mind and hardened himself to the new world he was forced to occupy. Endure was a better word, but he still had some choices, however limited. One of those was to leave the Gauntlet, which he did after casting a last wistful gaze up to his old apartment as he walked by on the rain-soaked and trash-strewn street.

After making his way to the nearby Dominion Docks, only to find them even less hospitable than the Gauntlet, Michael reversed course and headed for the city centre, where he hoped the pickings would be richer. Luck was with him the first few times as he artfully extracted wallets and purses from pockets and handbags. However, Michael quickly learned that the little-to-non existent police presence in the Gauntlet did not apply the closer you came to the financial hub of the Golden Gateway or the historic Imperial Mile. He only managed to evade arrest by the skin of his teeth.

Deciding that discretion was the better part of valour, Michael opted to abandon the city centre and continue to the wealthy suburbs of Green Haven to scout for opportunities. He was not naïve and knew that a skinny, grimy street urchin would stick out among the picket fences and manicured lawns of the residential neighbourhoods or the upscale boutiques and salons of the shopping districts. So, he became a creature of the night, discretely sleeping where he could during the day and making Green Haven his playground after sunset. Raiding the dumpsters behind supermarkets yielded more than enough food just past its sell-by date. On occasions, he even found clothing that loosely fit. One jackpot offered a partially damaged tent, good enough for Michael to set up camp in the forested outskirts of some parkland.

Eventually, as life became less about simply surviving, boredom and curiosity got the better of him. Michael would peer through windows during his nightly wanderings to observe families living their lives. As befitted Green Haven, the children would want for nothing. Michael could sometimes get so close without being noticed, that he smelt the dinner the families would sit down to. He could watch the video games the children played after the meal or the movies the adults relaxed in front of once the young ones had been put to bed. He would sometimes imagine being part of such a family and quickly admonish himself for foolish sentimentality.

One evening, he spotted an ornate mansion on the grounds of a large estate. From a distance, it looked luxurious. Multiple sports cars were parked out front, and a tennis court and pool nestled amid a vast garden tended by a dozen groundsmen. For all the fine-living Michael had observed in other typical suburban neighbourhoods, this was on another level. He reasoned that whoever owned it must be powerful, and not simply because of the wealth on display. As well as groundsmen and servants going about their domestic duties, Michael spotted numerous imposing guards wearing matching black suits with shades. They reminded him of the stories he had heard of the close protection agents of the Imperial Guard, sworn to protect the Royal family and political leaders, or die trying. Doubtless, the estate guards would also be carrying concealed weapons.

Nevertheless, Michael challenged himself to find a way onto the grounds and explore the mansion. At worst, he would satisfy his curiosity about how the gilded elite lived. At best, he might find something valuable that he could take and exchange for a few hundred sovereigns. It would easily be enough to pay for a few nights in a warm bed after a hot bath.

Michael spent days carefully scouting the perimeter of the estate, assessing potential entry points over the walls, as well as climbing tall trees to get a sense of the layout. He found a blind spot for the numerous security cameras and noted the guards' patrol patterns. Nighttime was now his natural habitat, and with his clothing already dark and grimy, Michael would easily blend in. Then, as he arrived at his favourite vantage point to await an opportune moment on his chosen night, he found the estate transformed. Party music blared, thousands of helium-filled balloons were anchored to the ground, and multicoloured lights painted the mansion's exterior. Michael spotted hundreds of guests mingling in and around the house, helping themselves to champagne offered on silver trays and gorging on food beautifully arranged on long buffet tables.

Whatever the reason for the celebration, Michael saw it not as an inconvenience but an opportunity. With so many new people about, after they left or retired for the night, anything out of the ordinary would not be easily spotted by the guards. While still needing to be cautious, it meant that Michael would not have to watch every single step or leave items seemingly untouched. Additionally, there was no way that so much food could be consumed, which meant there would be plenty of leftovers for him to pillage.

Michael waited patiently for hours, shifting his position upon the high tree branch from time to time. Eventually, the party wound down. The majority of the guests left in their chauffeur-driven luxury vehicles, while the privileged few retired to what were presumably guest rooms on the upper floors of the house. The mansion grounds looked like a bomb had gone off in a party goods store, and Michael didn't envy the cleanup crew the next morning.

He checked his stolen watch. There were still a few hours until dawn, more than enough time to sneak in and out. Michael carefully inched his way along the tree branch until he was over the wall, lowered himself so that he hung with both arms for a moment, and dropped.

Michael silently entered the kitchen through the back door. He had always intended it as his way into the mansion. However, the party aftermath forced him into a few detours along the way to avoid lingering guards, given their usual patrol routes had been disrupted. He quietly closed the door behind him and scanned the room as best he could in the gloom. Michael had pretty good natural night vision, but the decorative lighting on the grounds had caused him to lose a little on the way over. He paused until it improved and, while doing so, indulged the curiosity that was one of the reasons for his visit. The kitchen was predictably huge, all dark polished marble and carved wooden cupboards. He opened a few and found several tins of salmon and caviar, which he dropped into his bag, eager to later try something he had never sampled. If that was just what the cupboards provided, then surely the fridge would offer even greater delights?

Michael weighed up the loss of night vision that would come from exposure to the inner fridge light versus the rare opportunity to savour delicacies beyond his reach. Foraging for food in supermarket dumpsters was all very well for getting hold of the basics, but he couldn't remember the last time he had consumed anything vaguely chilled, even milk. He reasoned that he could explore the mansion and raid the fridge on his way back out, but temptation quickly overcame reason, and he opened it.

At first, the light was blinding and consumed Michael, for the fridge was taller than he was. He closed his eyes but gradually opened them, his pupils' adjusting. He couldn't help but gaze in awe at what he saw. It was as if he had not just opened a fridge but the gate to a garden of unearthly delights. He was dazzled at the assortment of foods, from cooked meats to fish to fruit juices, all eclipsed by a collection of indulgent desserts. His eyes were drawn to a large bowl of chocolate mousse, shaped into a soft peak with a succulent strawberry perched at the summit. He plucked the strawberry and popped it into his mouth whole. He crushed it between his teeth and savoured the sweet juice. All the fruit he had salvaged had been on the cusp of rotting, and even those berries he managed to find in nature were small and often bitter.

His gaze returned to the mousse. Michael debated opening a drawer to find a spoon but thought better of it. He was here to get in and out with what he could, not indulge in gourmet dining. Michael raised his forefinger and used it to carve a deep groove in the mousse, like a digger scooping up earth. He quickly stuck his finger in his mouth and sucked on it. If the strawberry had been exquisite, then the mousse was divine. Michael couldn't help but close his eyes and attempt to commit the taste to memory so he could do his best to relive the sensation in future.

'Chocolate is nice, but I prefer strawberry flavour,' came a voice from behind him.

Michael snapped his eyes open and spun around. He was confronted by a young girl with raven hair, clothed in a white silk nightdress. The light from the fridge combined with the dress to give her an almost ghostly quality, though she was so pretty that angelic was a better descriptor. Taken aback by the sight, Michael stumbled into the fridge, causing the glass and crockery containers inside to rattle noisily.

'It's okay,' said the girl soothingly as she held a hand up for Michael to be calm. 'You don't need to be scared. No one's going to hurt you.'

Michael's heart raced. He reflexively looked at the rear kitchen door and the escape it offered.

'Do you want something to eat?' the girl asked gently. Given that he was the intruder in her house, Michael thought it odd that she was the calmer one.

She slowly approached the fridge. Michael backed away. The girl reached in, grabbed the bowl of mousse and took it to a nearby kitchen island, using the ambient light provided by the fridge to find her way. She opened a drawer, pulled out a dessert spoon and set it down next to the bowl.

'You can finish it if you like,' she offered, nodding down to the mousse. 'No offence, but I don't think anyone else would want it after where your finger has probably been.'

She smiled, indicating that her remark was a gentle tease rather than a criticism. Michael again eyed the rear door. He was prepared to bolt, but her next words stopped him.

'Please stay,' the girl said.

There was something in her voice that Michael found soothing, comforting even. As the adrenaline of his initial surprise began to fade, his instinct to flee was replaced by the one that had originally brought him to her door and beyond it; that of curiosity.

He cautiously set down his backpack and stepped over to the kitchen island. The girl must have registered his trepidation. She slowly moved away from the mousse, leaving him to fill the space she had just occupied while she rounded the island and stood opposite him.

'My name's Sarah,' she said. 'What's yours?'

'Michael,' he replied flatly as he eyed the mousse.

'Nice to meet you, Michael. Welcome to my house. Well, technically, it's my dad's house. It was his birthday today. That's what the party was for.'

Michael kept staring at the mousse, not seeming to hear her.

'Go on, dig in,' Sarah urged. 'Something like that is meant to be enjoyed.'

Michael took her at her word, grabbed the spoon and started shovelling mousse into his mouth.

'Whoa!' she exclaimed in amusement. 'Slow down, or you'll get sick.'

He looked up to her and paused, chocolate smeared around his mouth.

'Sorry,' he said. 'I always eat quickly. Never know when someone might take it from you.'

'That sounds awful,' said Sarah, concerned.

'That's life,' retorted Michael with a shrug. He continued eating but at a more considered pace.

'How old are you?' probed Sarah.

'Thirteen, I think,' replied Michael.

'You think? What, you mean you don't know?'

'I know the day, just a little fuzzy on the year. My mother would know, but she's not here.'

'Where is she?' Sarah queried.

Michael replied with a silent shrug.

'Oh,' said Sarah gently. 'That's two things we have in common, then.'

'Two?' he asked.

'I'm thirteen as well,' she said. 'And my mother isn't here either. Actually, sorry, I didn't think. I mean she died a couple of years ago. She's gone, but I do know where she is, out at the burial gardens. So, I guess it's just the one thing we have in common then.'

'Probably the only thing, too,' said Michael sardonically. 'This is your world, Sarah. I don't belong in it. Thanks for the dessert.'

He dropped the spoon into the now-empty bowl with a clatter, picked up his backpack and made for the kitchen door.

'Wait,' she said urgently. Michael paused and turned. 'I can think of at least one other thing we have in common.'

'What's that?' he asked sceptically.

'We're both alone,' Sarah replied.

She slowly walked up to him and laid a tender hand on his arm.

'Before she passed, my mother would often say that you could never have too much kindness in the world. You're right, I do live in a bubble, but I'm not stupid either. I know how harsh it can be out there. But you don't just know it; you live it. So, how can I let you leave without at least offering to help?'

Michael rattled his backpack.

'I've got your fish.'

Sarah grinned.

'I think I can do a little better than that. Stay here tonight. There are plenty of guest rooms. Wash up, sleep in a proper bed, have a decent breakfast, and leave with clean clothes.'

Michael gazed at her, mulling over what to do.

'Does that really seem so bad compared to what's out there?' she asked.

Suddenly, now that she was so close and not half-concealed in shadow, the combination of Sarah's glowing smile and beautiful eyes hit Michael. A spark lit a fire inside him, and from that moment onwards, he could think of nothing else but her. She could have offered him a pile of straw in the stables, and he would have felt eternally grateful.

Michael slowly nodded.

'Thanks,' he said as he raised his own smile, the first in a very long time.

'No problem,' said Sarah. 'But if you're going to be a guest here, then we should do this properly.' She extended a hand for him to shake. 'Sarah Trelane, pleased to meet you.'

He took her hand and gently shook it.

'Michael Ryan. Pleasure's all mine.'

Michael promised himself that even though it would only be one night under her roof, he would spend as long as it took to vindicate Sarah's faith in him. For years he would try, and for years, he would fail.

Twelve Years Later

1

PASSING THE TORCH

Michael looked down upon the mansion grounds and the preparations for the birthday celebrations. Little had changed, except now he had a view of proceedings from the balcony of his room rather than a tree branch. There were fewer buffet tables and catering staff, as befitted the smaller guest list compared to the night he snuck in. In part, the reduced numbers were due to many of Charlie Trelane's past associates either ending up in prison or dead. Both he and Michael knew it was also a result of the decline in power and influence of House Trelane.

It was still foremost among the Crime Families, but all champion racehorses eventually slowed until it was time to retire. Michael could tell Charlie was getting close, that he lacked the drive and ambition of even a few years prior. The old crime boss had become more magnanimous towards his opponents following the death of his wife, Elizabeth, as if in a display of penance. However, he had only grown despondent since Sarah had left. Mercy and misery were not the best qualities to remain at the top of Dominion City's ruthless criminal hierarchy.

Michael retreated into his room and stood before the main mirror. He smoothed his tuxedo and straightened his bowtie. He could barely associate himself with the scruffy, stringy and morose street rat he had once been. Over a decade of decent food, quality education and kind treatment had worked wonders. His dedication to physical fitness had taken care of the rest, shaping a physically powerful young man with a calm yet confident manner. Yet, Michael never forgot where he came from and how easily it could be snatched away. It perhaps explained his reticence growing up in the Trelane household. In contrast, his peers who were born and bred within the opulence of the other Houses were loud, brash and reeked of privilege.

It helped that Sarah was by Michael's side for much of that time, first as his salvation, then as his friend and, eventually, as his lover. He turned away from the mirror and gazed at a framed photograph of her in adulthood that rested on the mantlepiece. Michael was as lost in her eyes now as during that night in the kitchen. He turned away. There was no point dwelling on the past. It only led to pain. Michael needed to focus on the future. He checked his watch. He was wanted in Charlie's study. The future was precisely what the old man wanted to talk about.

Michael made his way along the polished wooden corridor in the direction of Charlie's study. Despite passing the displays for years, he still occasionally glanced at the various suits of armour belonging to knights of the early Everlight Imperium that lined the walls. Mixed in with them were warrior outfits from countries around the world, whether the bulky fur robes, iron plating and double axe of a berserker from Kreigvoss or the ornate armour and bejewelled blade of a Dragon Guard warrior from Haikuza. Military history was not the sole focus for Charlie. The entire mansion could have easily doubled as a museum of all things, and scholars would have given anything for just a few days access to the library. The head of House Trelane was a man of simple tastes. However, he liked to feel connected to the past, reinforcing his belief that he was carving out his own little slice from the grand history of Dominion City.

Michael paused halfway down the corridor, convinced he had caught something in the corner of his eye trying to remain concealed behind a display. Before he could turn, he suddenly felt lithe arms come from behind to wrap around his waist and slowly ascend to caress his chest.

'Hello handsome,' came the seductive female voice, all tease and no innocence.

Michael rolled his eyes and instantly knew who had ambushed him. He gently took the bare arms and pulled them away. He turned around to find Sinderella Huxley facing him, biting her lower lip and eyeing him with barely concealed desire. With clear porcelain-white skin, flowing blonde hair, and an elegant ball gown that complemented her lean figure, there was no doubt that Sinderella was a beauty. Unfortunately, the mind that occupied the shell belonged to a beast. She had tried for years to seduce Michael, but he never succumbed to her charms, even at his lowest point after Sarah walked out. Like most men, he had been tempted. Unlike most, he knew of Sinderella's sadistic streak, which, matched by unstable psychology, was a combination ripe for disaster. It surprised Michael that she was never committed to an institution. However, he suspected Sinderella's brother of managing to talk Charlie out of any such action.

'What do you want, Sindy?' asked Michael wearily, knowing what the answer was, having batted away her attentions more times than he could remember.

'Same thing I have for years, Mikey,' she replied as she started sucking her thumb.

'And if you ever got it, I'd end up like a puppy a few days after Winterfest,' he retorted. 'Tossed away after you got bored, just like every other plaything.'

'No,' she said with a wounded tone as she feigned a pained expression. She leaned forward to whisper into Michael's ear. 'I'd never get bored of the fun we'd have.'

She started sucking on his earlobe, which he indulged for a moment until he felt teeth begin to clamp down. He shoved her away with ease.

'I haven't got time for this,' he snapped. 'Don't you have any small animals to torture instead?'

'Hey, a girl has to entertain herself any way she can,' Sinderella replied, sucking her thumb once more as if nothing had happened. 'I'm just looking forward to the main event.'

Michael knew she was referring to the show fight that would take place between him and her brother for the entertainment of the party guests. They had sparred over the years in the mansion gym, but Charlie had requested a public display for some reason. Who were they to turn down the birthday boy and, more to the point, the man to whom they owed everything?

'Really? You're looking forward to watching your brother have that smirk wiped from his pretty face?' Michael asked, seeking to provoke.

'Hardly,' Sinderella scoffed. 'You and I both know he could beat you handcuffed.'

'Well, I'm sure you have plenty to lend him.'

Sinderella smiled wickedly, fully grasping the inference made about her bedroom habits.

'You don't know what you're missing, Mikey,' she said in an unsettling sing-song way.

He pursed his lips and shrugged.

'I'd say when it comes to that, ignorance is bliss.'

Her smile dropped and was instantly replaced with a bitter glare. Michael ignored her and carried on towards Charlie's study.

Michael knocked gently on the study door and waited.

'Come!' he heard Charlie bellow.

He opened the door, walked through and closed it gently behind him. Michael saw Charlie standing behind his large marble desk, resting an arm on the back of a stylish wooden and velvet chair that more resembled a throne. Charlie, also dressed in a tuxedo, was turned away from the room and stared out a large window that looked down upon the mansion's main driveway. He removed a cigar from his mouth and blew a long plume of pungent smoke as Michael approached. For a moment, he simply stood there, his focus on the driveway rather than his guest. Charlie leaned forward slightly when the gates to the estate opened. A vehicle appeared, but he immediately lost interest when he saw it was a limousine belonging to yet another party guest.

'She's not coming, Charlie,' said Michael quietly.

Charlie huffed, turned and stubbed out the cigar in a gold ashtray that rested upon his desk.

'I know,' the old man croaked in his gravelly voice. 'You can't blame me for hoping, though, especially on my birthday.'

'She hasn't turned up for the last few,' noted Michael. 'Why would she come tonight?'

He hadn't said it to be mean, just to state the facts. Michael had always been respectful towards his benefactor ever since their first meeting when a sceptical Charlie agreed to take in the young homeless boy following Sarah's appeals. Yet Michael had never been a yes man, who only told Charlie what he wanted to hear. It was genuine respect that meant Michael always spoke truth to power because he hoped it would lead to better outcomes.

On several occasions, ever since his elevation to the inner circle of advisors, Michael's counsel successfully helped Charlie avoid potentially bloody and damaging feuds between House Trelane and its competitors. The Crime Families would never gather around a campfire and sing songs together. Still, there was a smart way of competing, through building alliances and profitable business ventures, and a stupid way, principally through the gun and the protection racket. Some who had Charlie's ear accused Michael of going soft and thus making House Trelane appear weak when shows of strength were the order of the day. Nevertheless, Charlie increasingly relied on Michael's advice. Whether it was the quality of that counsel or the old man's waning ruthlessness and lack of appetite for criminality that were the main influencers, Michael couldn't say.

Charlie sighed and sat upon his throne wearily. He started stroking his handlebar moustache, light grey like his hair. The leader of House Trelane came across as a man tired of life, which saddened Michael to see on what should have been the day to celebrate it.

'Yeah, I know. I just hoped she'd change her mind this one time. I even sent a letter askin' her to come. She probably didn't even open it.'

'What's so special about tonight?' asked Michael. 'Other than the obvious, of course.'

'I was going to announce my retirement,' said Charlie casually, as if he were revealing something far more trivial, such as what colour to repaint the dining room.

Michael raised his eyebrows in mild surprise, though he felt such a move had been coming sooner than later based on Charlie's recent despondency. The old man had offered little indication as to the timing, but his birthday and the accompanying ceremony made as good an occasion as any for the world to find out. Still, part of Michael's role was to challenge his boss's decisions.

'I have to be honest with you, Charlie-' began Michael.

'I'd expect nothin' less,' interjected the old man.

'You've not been yourself since she left.'

'You look in the mirror lately?' Charlie asked acidly.

'Plenty of times and I've looked away more than a few, too,' Michael retorted. 'But let me finish.'

Charlie grunted but nodded in acquiesce. Michael continued.

'Sarah broke our hearts. Maybe they needed breaking, I don't know. But it means we've been thinking more with them and less with our heads. In this business, that's not always the right move. I worry it's affecting your judgement, and this is one of those times.'

Charlie absorbed Michael's words. He rapped a knuckle on the wooden arm of his throne.

'I hear what you're sayin'. I understand it too and agree completely.'

Michael maintained a measured exterior but was slightly taken aback. Even when Charlie eventually came around to his way of thinking, he still put up token resistance to thoroughly test both sides of an argument before making a decision. He had never known Charlie to roll over so easily. The old man heaved himself up from his throne. He returned to staring pensively out the window as the sun set below the distant horizon, casting him in an eerie red glow.

'You're right. I 'ave been listenin' to my heart a lot more since Elizabeth died. How could I not, given what happened to her?' Charlie began. 'I know the risks and how it'll look to the other Houses, even inside this one. But it ain't an impulsive decision, Michael, made just 'cause I'm feelin' depressed. My head's also been tellin' me for a long time that it's the right thing to do, not just to retire as the head of the House, but to retire the House itself.'

Michael stepped forward, keen to make sure he wasn't misunderstanding Charlie.

'Are you-' he paused and corrected himself. 'Are *we* getting out of the game?'

Charlie turned to him, his expression serious. There was no room for misunderstanding.

'I am, but you're not, my boy,' the old man said with a weak smile. 'I'm not sure whether to congratulate you or commiserate, but without an heir, or at least one that wants any part of it, you're the natural choice to take over and make House Trelane a legitimate organisation, to do things properly.'

Michael wasn't sure what to say. He felt proud that Charlie had chosen him for such a task, but the swirl of thoughts as to the implications made it challenging to articulate a response.

'Huxley won't be happy,' was all he could muster, though he immediately chastised himself for not expressing gratitude first. But then was a simple 'thank you' adequate when he had just been handed an empire on a plate?

'Don't worry, I'll talk to him,' replied Charlie, dismissing the concern. 'The world isn't what it was, Michael. We're still only at the top 'cause we're big enough to be, 'cause of what I did to get us there. Well, it cost me enough too. Money will never be an issue again, and what good is power if you don't 'ave the will or the vision to use it? They're the only two things that matter in this business, and I just don't care anymore. You do, though, and you've got the patience, the smarts and the drive to do some good with it. It's time to end things while I can still make amends, to try and salvage things with Sarah before it's too late.'

'That's why you wanted her here tonight,' said Michael in realisation. 'To make the big reveal.'

Charlie sighed and nodded.

'Can you talk to her for me, let her know what I'm plannin', that I want to see her?' he asked.

'I can try,' Michael offered. 'But I doubt she wants to see me any more than she does you.'

'She will,' reassured Charlie. 'That girl was always on the lookout to save things, whether it was birds with broken wings or young, dirty street kids with broken lives. She hasn't changed.'

Charlie glanced at his watch and straightened his bowtie.

'We'd better go and greet our guests,' he continued. 'Don't say anything to anyone about our plans, especially you know who. I'll choose the right time.'

'I don't think there'll ever be a right time to tell Huxley the news,' said Michael. 'But don't worry, I won't say anything. He doesn't need any more of an excuse to want to beat me to a pulp.'

'Yeah, the big fight,' noted Charlie as if he had forgotten. 'Thanks for agreeing to that. There's a method to the madness. You win, and your stock will climb even higher in the House. It'll pave the way for you to take over from me.'

'And if I lose?' probed Michael cautiously, as if even raising the possibility contained peril.

Charlie placed a hand on Michael's shoulder and squeezed.

'Don't.'

2

HEIR APPARENT

Dominic Huxley stood before his own ornate mirror and observed himself. Unlike Michael's periods of self-reflection, these were exercises in pure vanity. Huxley was naked, all the better to admire the lean, sculpted physique he had spent years perfecting, with not a trace of fat. Complemented by a handsome face, slick dark hair, and piercing blue eyes, Huxley regarded himself as a prime physical specimen. The hundreds of women he had bedded and discarded thought so too.

Huxley flexed his biceps and revelled in their definition. He knew he looked good at all times but needed to especially impress for Old Man Trelane's party and, specifically, the show fight that would feature. Only Huxley had no intention of it being purely for show. Ever since their sparring sessions in the gym had tailed off, Huxley had waited for a legitimate reason to destroy Michael Ryan. Now that opportunity had arrived. Huxley had no idea why Charlie wanted to stage such an event. Still, he would take full advantage of it to cement his credentials - no, his *right* - to take over running House Trelane when the old fart finally stepped down or died.

Huxley was the heir to a House that no longer existed, so complete had been Charlie Trelane's destruction of what many in the criminal fraternity had regarded as a vicious upstart. House Huxley had not been unduly brutal, not in young Dominic's eyes. It had just been efficient. If there was an obstacle in your way, then you just cleared it as simply and effectively as possible. Should that result in hundreds of deaths, many admittedly innocent, that was unfortunate, but just business.

The other Houses hadn't seen it that way, however. Supposedly it brought too much attention, even from the usually pliable police department. Their grand, if temporary, alliance with Charlie at its head had ground House Huxley into dust, with the only two survivors being himself and Sinderella. It had been blind luck, with the twins out of Dominion City attending a West Coast boarding school, only to return to ruins. Though Huxley held Charlie's growing softness in contempt, he supposed he owed his life to the emergence of a conscience in the old man just in time to not only spare the young siblings but to take them into his house. Huxley had since dutifully declared fealty to Charlie, playing the long game until he could position himself to take the power that was rightfully his.

He had always been attracted to power, craved it even. He just couldn't explain what he would ever do with it once acquired. Huxley often regretted being born in the wrong century, feeling his spirit was more suited to the glories of imperial conquest and the ecstasy of battle. He was not interested in the politics of control, just in the act of gaining it and enforcing it upon lesser beings. Not only would they know defeat, but submit to it and acknowledge their error in even resisting in the first place. Such sentiments caused him to admire the collection of military uniforms and armour that lined the corridor to Charlie's study. However, his most prized possessions he kept hidden away, not just to enjoy them in private, but because they were strictly forbidden.

The movement known as Firestorm had briefly controlled the Everlight Imperium over a century ago, before their overthrow and the reform of the empire into a democracy. Huxley admired their militancy and dedication to the creed of flame, ridiculously labelled as heresy by the declining solar temples. Above all, he appreciated their cast iron will and determination. They had sought control and seized it without mercy, but only after exercising patience and careful planning. Huxley saw a lot of parallels to his own situation, though he was forced to wear suits rather than the jackboots and stylish black uniforms of Firestorm, with their red and yellow trimming and attractive peaked caps. He would sometimes parade in uniform in his secret chambers underneath the mansion, glorifying in the triumphal music that filled the air and rare illegal images of Firestorm in their prime projected onto the walls. He was sane enough to recognise it was pure fantasy. It would never be fulfilled, but what was the point of living if you couldn't chase your dreams?

Speaking of chasing unfulfilled dreams, Huxley had long resented Michael for stealing Sarah away from him. Not that she had ever actually been involved with Huxley or even aware of his interest in her, but that was beside the point. The upstart street urchin had appeared one day as a new member of the family without any kind of consultation. Huxley saw that Sinderella took an instant liking to Michael and had also spotted the early signs of Sarah's affection for him. Young Dominic, however, was alive to the threat the new competition presented to his status. So it proved, as Michael the golden boy gradually wormed his way into the apple of Charlie's eye and eventually into Sarah's bed, two places that were rightfully Huxley's to occupy. Such a slight would never be forgiven or forgotten. Still, if true vengeance would have to wait, then the gratification of inflicting violence upon Michael Ryan at the birthday brawl would suffice for the time being.

Sinderella opened Huxley's bedroom door without knocking and walked in, unperturbed by his nudity. She slammed the door behind her and stomped over to the luxurious bed, her heels clacking loudly on the polished marble floor. Huxley didn't turn but could see in the mirror that her face was thunderous, and so he was surprised to see her fling herself upon the bed and burst into tears rather than scream or rant. Sinderella bawled, her cries muffled by the thick duvet. Huxley rolled his eyes, no stranger to her theatrics. He knew his twin sister flirted dangerously with insanity but loved her anyway, perhaps a little too much at times.

He strode over to the bed, sat beside her and started gently running his fingers through her hair.

'What's wrong, Sin?' he gently probed. He also knew his pet name for her was more than apt given her tastes.

'It's Mikey,' Sinderella managed to croak between wails.

'What has that insufferable son of a bitch done now?' asked Huxley, annoyed at the mere mention of his nemesis.

Sinderella rolled onto her back and wiped her eyes, smearing mascara across the back of her hands.

'It's not what he's done. It's what he's *going* to do.'

'Get to the point,' ordered Huxley, his annoyance starting to transfer to his sister. Patience had never been one of his virtues, not that he had many in the first place.

'He's going to take over everything. Take it all away from us,' Sinderella blubbed.

'What are you talking about?'

'I snuck up to Charlie's study after seeing Mikey in the corridor. I heard them talking, so I wasn't going to miss the chance to listen in. Charlie said he's going to announce his retirement tonight and make Mikey his heir, to have the House quit the business and go legit. This whole fight tonight is supposed to be a way of building Mikey up. What are we going to do, Dommie?'

Huxley had listened to Sinderella's story with apparent calm, an occasional slow blink the only sign he was processing her words. Inside his head, however, fury erupted. Images of torture, mutilation and death filled his mind's eye, as well as fire; always fire. They were a comfort to him. The temptation to fly into a rage and smash anything within easy reach was overpowering. Still, Huxley forced himself not to yield to the impulse. As gratifying as it would have been, there was a far better moment to unleash his wrath and have it mean something.

Huxley stood and flexed his muscles, channelling his rage, infusing their fibres with the fire he felt inside. He looked down at his palms and realised he had squeezed his fists so hard that his nails had bitten into the skin and drawn blood.

'What are we going to do?' he repeated Sinderella's question. '*We* are doing nothing. If Charlie wants to build Michael up, then I will be the one to tear him down.'

3

RING OF FIRE

Michael was of the firm opinion that if there was a worse creature than Sinderella that occupied House Trelane, it was her twin brother. The pair were already ensconced at the mansion when Michael arrived, having been taken in by Charlie after he destroyed House Huxley. To his credit, such an action showed Charlie's magnanimity following his wife Elizabeth's death was not just for show. However, over the years, Michael came to feel, during his darker moments, that Charlie would have been more merciful, and done the world a bigger favour, if he had properly finished the job of wiping out the Huxleys.

The twins were poison, though they always presented loyal and saintly personas to Charlie. Huxley and Michael had quickly formed a visceral loathing for each other. For Huxley, Michael was the shiny new toy that threatened to usurp his position. Michael, for his part, could instantly sense the dark void that constituted Huxley's soul, having come to know the type during his early struggles in the Gauntlet. As Michael stared into Huxley's eyes across the duelling ring, he knew the soul into which they were a window was as black as ever.

A small circular arena had been constructed in the garden at the rear of the mansion. It was encompassed by a wire cage, the mesh clear enough to see through, and the surface had been elevated to afford the surrounding audience a good view of proceedings. Michael felt uneasy, like he had been transported back in time and place to the legendarily brutal gladiatorial blood pits of ancient Kreigvoss. The baying crowd did little to reassure him. Michael was not a naturally violent man, for he had grown sick of it after seeing and experiencing far too much in his youth. However, neither was he a stranger to brutality and combat. Both had been essential to his survival before being taken in by Charlie. Following the earlier meeting with his benefactor, it had become clear that tonight, though Michael's physical survival was not in question, his reputation was certainly on the line. In the criminal world he occupied, having the second undermined was a clear path to doubts forming over the first.

Michael tried to push his unease to the back of his mind and focus on the task at hand or, more accurately, the person. Huxley was dressed in a tight fitting yellow shirt with red streaks, his legs half covered by long black Lycra shorts. Michael was similarly dressed, except his top was black with red streaks. Both were barefoot. On the floor, close to each man, were placed a fighting staff, two billy clubs and a circular shield, all wooden. Michael certainly hadn't expected them to be made of foam, though it was rapidly dawning on him that this would not be some kind of fake fight for the crowd, but the real deal. The question was how far would each man go?

If Huxley's cheerleaders were any indication, he wouldn't be showing much restraint. Stood behind him, peering through the cage mesh, were Sinderella and Huxley's right-hand man, Gideon Lynch. The latter was a gaunt, wiry figure, indicating too much past or current drug use. Pale skin and delicately applied eyeliner gave him an Emo quality, complemented by a mop of unkempt jet-black hair that ensured a scruffiness that even his designer suit could not overcome. Lynch was not quite as vicious as his boss, but that wasn't saying much. His propensity for cruelty and violence made him the ideal enforcer, and though Michael had attempted to persuade Charlie to cut him loose, Huxley's influence had protected Lynch.

Michael may have won many battles, but not all of them. Though Charlie had indeed softened, it had only been from a very hard place, one which recognised the value of applied violence. Michael was no saint, and even if he did not endorse such methods, he still went along with them. That would all stop when he was in charge. But first there was the small matter of winning, and unlike Huxley with his evil-eyed supporters grinning with bloodlust, Michael had no-one in his corner.

To the side of the arena, a small platform had been erected, upon which was placed a throne for Charlie. Ever the king, the head of House Trelane sat upon it and considered the chanting crowd before him, building up their anticipation for the show to come. Michael noted that the morose self-reflection he had seen in Charlie a few hours previously had vanished, replaced with the confident grandiosity he was known for. Michael wondered if it was a mask Charlie was putting on in public, or whether he had suddenly rediscovered pleasure in his role and his supposed heir was about to receive a pummelling for no reason other than entertainment. Michael would find out soon. The plan was for Charlie to make his announcement after the fight concluded.

Charlie rose from his throne and raised and lowered his hands a few times, calling for quiet from the crowd, which duly obliged.

'Evenin' all. Firstly, thanks for comin'. It means a lot that my free food and booze are as big a draw as ever.'

The audience laughed at Charlie's attempt at wit, though Michael knew that their sycophancy would have guaranteed a positive reception no matter how poor the joke.

'But you know, there's always change, big and small,' he continued. 'That's just the nature of things, and our House ain't no different. Take these two fine young specimens.'

Charlie extended an arm and arced it from Michael to Huxley, highlighting them to the audience, who turned from the king to appreciate his knights.

'It's good to know that the future of House Trelane is in the hands of men like Michael and Dominic. They can appreciate the kind of changes that'll be needed for us to thrive in the years to come, and the new opportunities to be embraced. But there'll be just as many challenges to overcome as well. They'll need steel and fortitude, and so let's be in no doubt that they 'ave the metal to take on anythin' that comes their way. Now, 'cause you all know I like to spice things up a bit during these parties, Michael and Dominic have agreed to put on a little show. Get the blood pumping to see us through the rest of the night.'

With official acknowledgement of what they already knew was coming, the crowd started whooping with anticipation.

'Now, you know the rules boys. Fight fair, with no cheap shots to the brain, eyes, or the balls. Otherwise, 'ave at it, and show the world that House Trelane will be no pushover whatever the future holds.'

The crowd roared and Charlie sat, retrieved his customary lit cigar from a side table and observed Michael through narrowed eyes. He could almost read the old man's mind. *I've set them up for the big reveal, now don't make a mess of it.* Somewhere in the background, whether it was the real thing or pumped through a stereo system, Michael heard the beat of drums. They made a deep, pounding sound, likely to rile up ancient warriors before charging into battle. Michael couldn't fault the theatricality of the whole thing, and he was in no doubt who was playing the hero and the villain in this particular production.

Michael considered his options as to which weapon to go with, but the choice was made for him when Huxley, who had been staring intensely throughout Charlie's speech, suddenly launched forwards and scooped up the nearby wooden fighting staff as he went. The arena was perhaps twice the size of a typical boxing ring, and it took Huxley only seconds to close the distance to his opponent. Michael fixed a toe under his own staff, sharply lifted his leg to launch the weapon into the air, and caught it mid-flight. He held it tightly with both hands horizontally above his head as Huxley brought his own staff down vertically with lightning speed, the two weapons creating a loud but hollow clack as they impacted against each other.

The ferocity of Huxley's opening assault allowed Michael no room for doubt that his enemy was playing for keeps. Had Michael not deflected the blow in time, Huxley's staff would have split his head open. But what could he do? Ask for a pause, complain to the non-existent referee that Huxley already wasn't playing fair, and take his toys home? That would really cement his leadership credentials to the baying crowd. The whole subtext of Charlie's speech had been that his successor would guide the House to prosperity through good times and bad, and that Michael could defend against potential adversaries during and after the transition to legitimacy. Well, if Huxley was prepared to take things to the next level, then Michael would gladly meet him there.

An instant after his downward attack had been blocked, Huxley pivoted the base of his staff upwards, but Michael brought his one down to knee level to continue blocking. Both retreated a step to pull their staffs back and swing them in an arc towards each other. Both weapons clashed again with a clack, forming an X shape. Huxley rapidly sidestepped, flattened his staff parallel to his hip, and thrust it towards Michael's midriff. Michael flicked the lower half of his staff to parry away

Huxley's jab. However, Huxley went with the momentum and twirled clockwise with a full rotation.

Before he could block the move, Michael received the full blow to his right side. The pain was immediate and he figured that one or two ribs had at the very least been bruised, perhaps even cracked. He would have to worry about that later, though. Huxley had been continuously on the offensive since the start and Michael had only been reactive. He needed to change things up and regain the initiative.

Michael started to rapidly spin his staff, protecting his front from Huxley's exploratory jabs. Each time Huxley thrust forward, Michael jumped back. To the casual observer it looked like he was in constant retreat, backing off in fear. What Michael knew, however, was that he was deliberately encouraging overconfidence in his opponent. By thinking the advantage was his, Huxley focused on trying to find a way through Michael's spinning defence, sacrificing awareness of his surroundings. With each jump back, Michael had slowly pivoted towards his billy clubs and wooden shield on the ground. As he reached them, he abruptly stopped his defensive spinning and swung his staff towards Huxley's head. Michael knew his opponent would duck and counter. He preempted a sweeping kick from Huxley by jumping up.

Catching Huxley by surprise, Michael released his staff horizontally in a downward direction. It hit Huxley's nose, which exploded with blood, and left him sprawled on the arena floor. Michael landed back on his feet, crouched, and picked up both billy clubs. He twirled them stylishly, which he knew was pure showboating, but the crowd roared its approval that the fight was not as one sided as it seemed only seconds before.

Michael's confidence was high. He'd been one-nil down when Huxley had landed a blow to his ribs, but had clawed things back to a draw and left his nemesis's pretty face worse for wear. Michael caught a brief glimpse of Sinderella wailing and Lynch screaming profanities at him, and admitted to a sly satisfaction. Now it was time to finish things, to put Huxley in his place and show the party guests that there was soon to be a new boss in town, one worthy of respect, and who Huxley would be in no position to challenge.

Michael began striding with purpose towards a recovering Huxley, who wiped copious blood from his nose. He glared at Michael with unrestrained hatred and bared gritted teeth, themselves strained crimson. As Michael approached and raised his clubs, Huxley, still on his knees, did the unexpected and launched himself forward into a rolling dive. Whether by luck or design, Huxley timed it perfectly so that he was halfway through the roll as he found himself in front of Michael, and used the peak momentum of the motion to kick out with both feet simultaneously.

Huxley's soles hit Michael's solar plexus and hoofed him into the air. Michael went flying and hit the arena surface hard, completely winded. However, he had no time to catch his breath as he saw Huxley rise up and swing his staff downwards. Michael rolled to the side and missed the staff by inches as it slammed into the ground with a loud snap that left his ears ringing.

As he struggled to his feet, Michael tried to shake off the daze and fully expected Huxley to press the advantage. Instead, he saw his opponent flash a wicked, bloody smile, turn to Lynch, and nod. Lynch returned the evil grin. That couldn't be good. The henchman produced a lighter from his jacket pocket, flicked it open, sparked it up, and held the flame to where the base of the wire mesh met the arena floor. Fire instantly ignited and started to spread in both directions. Within seconds a circle of flame had enclosed the arena, much to the audience's shock and delight. It was waist-high and so still afforded the spectators a largely unimpeded view of the duel.

If Huxley had signalled to Lynch to initiate their little pyrotechnic display, then it wasn't something Charlie had sanctioned. Undoubtedly, it was intended as a nasty surprise, and it was likely Lynch had laced the borders of the arena with some kind of fire accelerant during the party preparations. Huxley's right-hand man glorified in the show, while Sinderella clapped ecstatically. Michael suddenly felt rage bubble up inside him. He knew he needed to maintain calm, to carefully study Huxley's strategy and come up with his own to counter it. Yet, Michael could not dampen the fire that rose within him as intensely as did the surrounding flames. He not only wanted to make Huxley pay, but to suffer, and in doing so also wipe the smiles from Lynch and Sinderella.

Michael released a furious battle cry and launched himself at Huxley. He pummelled with the billy clubs from every angle he could think of and with as much speed as he could muster, but each blow was blocked and deflected by Huxley's deft handling of his staff. It was almost as if he wasn't even trying, like a much bigger kid effortlessly holding a smaller one at arm's length while the latter repeatedly swung at thin air. It was then that Michael realised that Huxley always had the measure of him, that his nemesis had been sandbagging the whole time, hiding the extent to which he had refined his fighting skills since their gym sparring sessions had ended. Michael's fit of rage had only served to speed up his fatigue and cloud his thinking.

Huxley jumped back and, to the audience's delight, snapped his staff in half across a raised thigh to create two makeshift billy clubs of his own. So armed, he smirked and launched his own assault. Michael tried to parry as many of the blows as he could, but such was Huxley's speed that the inevitable happened and the punishment Michael's hands and knuckles took forced him to drop his clubs. Without defences, Michael was left wide open. Gripping a makeshift club, Huxley used an already clenched fist to slam Michael's jaw with such force that he spun several times on his way to hitting the floor. Seeing stars, Michael did the only thing that his scrambled mind could think of and crawled towards the wooden shield, the last remnant of the pile he had started with. He picked it up and used it to protect himself from the repeated blows Huxley landed with his clubs.

Whether out of tiredness or frustration, Huxley eventually desisted, threw his clubs aside, and tore the shield from Michael's grasp. He reached down to grab Michael's throat, but in a last act of defiance the latter kicked Huxley's legs out from under him, sending the nearly victorious villain crashing down. It was clear that both men were spent, but as they grappled and rolled over each other on the floor, Huxley had just enough wind in his sails to retain the upper hand. He managed to pin Michael down and punched his adversary in the face several times before Michael was able to land a return blow right on Huxley's bloody nose. As Huxley cried out in pain, Michael grabbed his enemy by the shirt collar and pulled him to the left, rolling Huxley onto his back. Michael used the momentum to get himself on top, effectively reversing their positions.

Michael landed several blows to Huxley's ribs, but with a roar Huxley forced both knees up and sent

Michael flying forward. He hit the floor, rolled and just about managed to stop burying his head into the flaming base of the wire mesh. Huxley was on him in seconds and Michael felt his face being pushed closer to the flames. Huxley clearly had the dominant position, using his weight to increase the downward pressure beyond Michael's ability to match it with upward resistance. Inch by inch, he felt the intensity of the heat increase against his face and eyes. Then, just as it was starting to become unbearable, Michael felt Huxley lean in behind his ear.

'Feel the burn,' he whispered gleefully.

Michael closed his eyes rather than be blinded. Doubtless he would be badly burned as Huxley shoved his face into the flames. Every time he looked in the mirror in future would be a reminder of his defeat and humiliation. His assumption of power in House Trelane would forever be associated with weakness. Blood would be in the water from the very beginning and the sharks would circle.

'Enough!' Charlie bellowed.

At first the agonising drive toward the flames did not cease, but after a moment Michael felt the pressure ease and he was free to push himself away. He turned and looked up to see a smug Huxley towering above, his point made without need to disobey Charlie's command. Huxley raised his arms in triumph and the crowd roared its approval. It certainly had been a show, just not one with the intended outcome.

Michael winced at the chill as Charlie's guards unleashed the contents of several fire extinguishers, but he was glad of the cooling effect as the nearby flames were doused. With the fire gone, Michael was able to clearly see Charlie through the mesh. He had risen from his throne, but whatever concern had caused him to call time on the duel was no longer apparent. The only expression on his face was one of disappointment. As their eyes met for a moment, Michael acknowledged the obvious and looked away. There would be no passing of the torch that night.

On the outskirts of the Trelane estate, close enough for a clear view of the fight that had just concluded, but far enough away not to be noticed, a shadowy figure perched upon the thick branch a young Michael Ryan had once used to clear the perimeter wall. Unlike Michael, the figure did not drop to the ground, but retreated into the darkness of night, as if it had never been there at all.

4

COFFEE AND REGRET

Michael tentatively touched his jaw. It had been a week since Huxley's fist had slammed into it, but it was still tender. The hot sweet coffee Michael sipped helped distract from the other aches and pains spread across his body. The general atmosphere of Sam's Coffee Emporium was soothing in itself. It was close enough to the financial centre of the Golden Gateway and the theatre and nightclub district of the Isle of Dreams to be classy, but Sam ensured it did not suffer from pretentiousness.

The dark wooden tables, plush armchairs, and antiques and old books placed upon shelves and dressers were all delicately illuminated by soft lighting and the glow of a roaring fire at the rear of the room. All that was missing was some breed of hunting dog dozing near the hearth. It was a favourite haunt of Michael's when he needed a quiet place to cast his mind adrift and watch the world go by. He especially liked it when it rained, or the snows of winter fell, and Sam's became a sanctuary against the elements, so cozy you could almost wrap yourself in it like a warm blanket.

Despite the comfort it usually provided, on this occasion the inviting atmosphere could not ease Michael's anxiety. The knot in his stomach had started tightening as soon as he entered and now, so close to the top of the hour, it was getting worse. He knew he should have timed it to arrive at the same moment as Sarah. It would have been easier to just throw himself into the encounter without over-thinking things beforehand. However, he decided to arrive early, to find a good table with two comfortable chairs, and allow himself time to consider what he would say. Michael and Sarah had often come to Sam's. He hoped that the positive memories associated with the place would make their reunion easier, but he knew that such hope was probably forlorn.

A year had passed since his last meeting with Sarah. It had not been the easiest of partings. Following her return from university, where she easily excelled in studying law, she had gradually cast off the cloak of naïvety wrapped around her since youth. After almost two years working for a prestigious law firm undertaking lucrative but unsatisfying corporate case work, Sarah surprised everyone, except perhaps Michael and Charlie, by quitting to take a low paid job as a community organiser in the Gauntlet. As Charlie said, Sarah always had a weakness for those in need, a legacy of her mother's teachings and her own intrinsic good nature. However, proximity to the harsher sides of Dominion City exposed Sarah to the role that House Trelane and the other Crime Families had in exploiting the downtrodden. Sarah's love for her father slowly gave way to unease, then discontent, and eventually to outright condemnation of his criminal lifestyle.

It increasingly became a source of tension between her and Michael. He owed everything to Charlie for taking him in and saving a young orphan from a harsh, brutal and, all too probably, short life. In an angry moment he called out Sarah's hypocrisy. Where did she think the money for her privileged upbringing and expensive education came from? Unsurprisingly, instead of pouring oil on troubled waters, it only added fuel to the fire. Despite the increased tension, their romance endured. The depth of their affection meant they felt they could overcome any obstacle, or so Michael thought until Sarah found her mother's lost letters. With the revelations they contained, everything changed and Sarah could simply no longer accept her life as she had known it.

She asked Michael, practically pleaded with him, to leave with her, for them to abandon their life so far and start a new one together. However, Michael's sense of duty and honour, of loyalty to Charlie, meant that he could not simply abandon the old man, especially with Huxley circling around the margins like some nefarious spectre. Michael asked for time to see what he could do to change things, but Sarah had none to give. She wanted out. It was a straight choice and he had chosen. Michael felt aggrieved at such a black and white interpretation. It was unfair, but then he knew all too well how unfair life was. Perhaps it had been that anger that fuelled his stubbornness in not reaching out to Sarah earlier. He had debated when and how to do so over the past year, indeed whether he even should, but Charlie's request had been the spur.

Michael's last memory of Sarah was of her walking away, her raven hair blowing in the wind as she wiped a hand across her face, presumably clearing away tears kept in check until he could no longer see her face. Now, as she walked through the main entrance into Sam's, she had no desire to hide herself. She scanned the room and quickly locked eyes with Michael, who instantly forgot whatever loose jumble of words he had come up with to greet her. Her hazel eyes were as penetrating as ever, her skin glowing, but Michael could tell that a certain weariness had set in. Her general demeanour had hardened a little. He was not surprised. The Gauntlet eventually ground everyone into dust, even the most resilient, let alone someone as previously sheltered as Sarah. It was to her credit that she had not simply abandoned her mission after a few weeks and returned to the plush certainties of the law chambers.

Michael stood as she approached. How should he greet her? A kiss? Too intimate. A handshake? Too formal. He settled on the middle ground of a gentle if awkward hug. Sarah stiffened slightly. They exchanged lukewarm smiles.

'Hi,' said Michael, unable to think of anything more profound. 'It's good to see you.'

'You too,' replied Sarah as she set her handbag down and took the free armchair opposite him.

Noticing the arrival of a new customer, Sam Bottom, the owner, approached bearing a broad smile that was anything but lukewarm. Short, wiry, and bespectacled, Sam always brought a bright mood that helped lift his customers' energy as much as the caffeine. Having greeted Michael earlier, Sam focused on the new arrival.

'Sarah! It's so good to see a familiar face. We've missed you.'

'Thank you Sam, I've missed you too.'

'But I bet you've missed my deluxe hot chocolate even more, yes?' he teased.

'I shouldn't,' said Sarah reluctantly.

'But you know her so well,' interjected Michael. 'She'll have one, and I'll have another latte, please Sam. Put them on my tab.'

'Sure thing,' replied Sam as he parted with a smile and returned to the barista area behind the counter.

Sarah looked back to Michael and considered him a moment. He felt a little unsettled.

'What?' he asked self-consciously.

'It may be good to see you, but you're not looking so good,' she replied.

Michael realised Sarah was referring to his fading black eye. He had become so used to it over the preceding days as to forget about it.

'Oh, yeah,' he said sheepishly. 'I was the main attraction at your dad's birthday party.'

'Excuse me?' Sarah queried. 'How do you mean?'

'What, that your dad had a party, or I was the main attraction?'

'I know very well he had his birthday. I got the letter he sent,' she replied tersely.

'Did you read it?'

'I did not, but don't avoid the subject. What about that eye?'

'Huxley and I put on a show for the guests. I'd have been happy with an air guitar duel, but you've got to give the masses what they want,' he replied, attempting to inject a little levity.

'You and Dominic went at it!' said Sarah, shocked. 'For what crazy reason?'

'Your father requested it,' replied Michael, suddenly serious again. 'He wanted… well, he wanted it to be part of the handover, to set me up in good standing with the rest of the House. It didn't quite work out that way.'

'Michael, every answer you're giving me just raises more questions,' said Sarah, exasperated. 'What handover?'

'You'd have an idea if you'd read Charlie's letter,' stated Michael, bluntly.

'I don't want anything to do with his world anymore,' she said softly, averting her eyes.

'You opened *my* letter,' he noted. 'The one I sent to your office. Otherwise we wouldn't be here right now.'

'I was intrigued,' she replied. 'Dad wouldn't have sent another so soon, and hardly anyone except him addresses me as Sarah Trelane these days.'

'What is it now? Are you married?' Michael blurted without thinking, genuinely surprised.

Sarah couldn't help but smile, amused.

'It's Ross, my mother's maiden name. Anyway, come on, what handover are you talking about?'

Michael took a deep breath and plunged in.

'Charlie's giving it up, Sarah. He's done with the life and walking away. He wants to make things up with you while he still can. He's leaving the House in my care, to reform it, to make it legitimate.'

Sarah stared blankly for a moment. Michael was unsure whether to add anything, but there wasn't really much more to reveal. Thankfully Sam appeared with their drinks to break the silence. He could tell it was best not to linger and gently set the small tray upon the table, nodded and retreated. Sarah reached down, picked up her hot chocolate and considered it a moment as she slowly stirred the whipped cream topping into the thick brown liquid.

'Why now?' she asked.

'The exact reason is for him to say. I wasn't totally surprised though. He's been distracted lately, losing focus. He doesn't seem to care like he used to. If I'm honest I think you breaking away was what did it. But even before that, I've seen him change over the years, soften.'

'Soften, really?' scoffed Sarah. 'The man with a stone heart? What, does he order people just to be maimed now, instead of killed?'

'Not on my watch,' Michael replied sternly. 'He listens to me. We do things the smart way. I guess that's why he wants me to take over.'

'Why are you defending him?' protested Sarah. 'You know what he's done.'

'I don't judge. I know how hard that world is,' Michael retorted defensively.

'Spare me that crap. You've spent more years in comfort than you did on the streets.'

'He gave me that shelter. He saved my life, Sarah.'

'And I suppose I had nothing to do with it,' she remarked coolly.

'That's not what I meant.'

Sarah paused a moment and set down her teaspoon.

'You know, you were right, what you told me before we split,' she said. 'I *was* a hypocrite.'

'I was angry when I said that. I didn't mean it,' replied Michael regretfully.

'Yes, you did, and rightly so. I enjoyed all the fruits of my dad's labour and then questioned it while still drinking from that cup. But what was even more unforgivable was how I could look at the people I was trying to help in the eye at the same time as men like my father were exploiting their suffering to make a quick sovereign. Walking away wasn't just the moral thing to do. It was the most honest. I live in a crummy apartment on the edge of the Gauntlet, where the hot water only works half the time and I carry a gun walking to and from work.'

'Sarah, that's not a safe place to-'

'And I wouldn't have it any other way, Michael. I'm close to people that need a hand to help them up, not a heel on their throats to keep them down. I don't live off anything associated with my father. I have my salary, my inheritance from my mother, and her good name. The first two aren't much, but the third is priceless to me.'

Sarah's lip started to quiver and Michael could see she was struggling to hold back tears. She set down her untouched hot chocolate.

'What hurts the most, though, is not that you chose to stay with my father instead of coming with me. It's that you knew the truth about my mother and still made that choice.'

'Sarah, I…' Michael trailed off, completely at a loss for what to say.

The conversation hadn't gone the way he thought it would, not at all. What he hoped would be a warm reunion, perhaps with initial awkwardness, had started off promisingly but rapidly declined as Sarah's still-raw emotional scars became evident. In truth, Michael hadn't planned on getting much further than appealing for some reconciliation between father and daughter, whereupon he fully expected Sarah to storm out. He would reluctantly accept being collateral damage, the messenger being shot while most of the ire was focused on Charlie. Unpleasant, but manageable.

Instead, what was actually happening was so much worse. Sarah's anger may still have been directed at her father, but her pain very much fell upon Michael's shoulders. He briefly flashed back to twelve years previously, when he took Sarah's hand of friendship and promised himself he would vindicate her faith in him. He knew he had let her down repeatedly, and so failed to keep that promise many times over. But at that moment, as an errant tear rolled down Sarah's cheek and she closed her eyes rather than look at him, Michael finally grasped the extent of his betrayal of both her and himself.

Sarah wiped away the tear, picked up her handbag and stood.

'So, no. Tell my dad I won't be coming back. There will be no reconciliation. I'm not saying that to be stubborn or cruel. I still love him, but I can't help hating him too, if that makes any kind of sense. There are consequences for the choices we make. Some have to carry a price. This is his.'

Michael stood and stepped towards her, but she backed off. Did he repulse her so much?

'And mine?' he asked, already knowing the answer.

'Goodbye, Michael,' Sarah replied, her voice breaking despite her best efforts. 'Good luck with the House. The future is yours now.'

She turned and headed towards the exit.

'Sarah, wait!' Michael called after her, but did not pursue. He knew it would do no good. In truth, there hadn't even been a point in appealing to her, but it was better to say something, anything, than to just remain silent and watch her walk out of his life a second time.

As Sarah disappeared out the main door, Michael stepped over to the nearby window and wiped dew from the glass. He ignored the confused or concerned looks from the other customers as he tried to angle himself to gain sight of her, but she was already gone. As if the world itself sensed his mood, thunder cracked and a deluge of rain suddenly appeared from nowhere, soaking the street and those who walked upon it in seconds.

Michael continued staring out the window, his eyes focused downwards on a large puddle outside, the droplets causing continuous ripples. If the surface of the puddle had remained undisturbed enough to show a reflection, and if Michael had not been so lost in his thoughts, he may have spotted a glimpse of a shadowy figure perched high above on the opposite building, lurking among the stone gargoyles and having borne witness to Michael and Sarah's every word.

5

COUNCIL OF WAR

Michael drove back to the Trelane estate in a daze. When he parked his sports car in its usual spot, he couldn't even remember the route taken back from the city, so preoccupied had his mind been in churning over his meeting with Sarah. Michael sat for a moment in the car, pondering his next move as the rain continued to lash down, blocking any kind of view through the windows and creating the feeling of being cocooned. He didn't know how Charlie would react. With disappointment, certainly, but whether defiant anger or sullen acceptance would follow was anyone's guess. Michael had seen far more of the second lately, but Charlie had built both an empire and a reputation on the first. He hoped that if any such anger did manifest itself, it would be directed at him and not Sarah.

Michael waited a few minutes for the rain to ease, but when it became obvious that no such respite was coming, he pulled up the collar of his trench coat, reluctantly exited the car and ran for the main entrance to the mansion. As soon as he made it through into the grand hall, Michael removed his coat, handed it to an attentive maid and headed straight for Charlie's study. There was no sense procrastinating. Charlie knew Michael had been meeting Sarah and so would expect a report of events. Michael bounded up the ornate master staircase and weaved down several corridors, passing the display of warrior armour on his way to the study. He reached the door and tapped lightly. It took less than a second for Charlie to bellow an invitation to enter. Michael took a deep breath to calm his nerves and gingerly opened the door.

Expecting to see only Charlie, he was surprised to find Huxley, Lynch and half a dozen lieutenants forming a semi circle in front of Charlie's desk as the man himself occupied his throne, a smouldering cigar braced between two fingers. Michael could instantly tell that this was no casual meeting. It had the feeling of a council of war.

'What's going on?' asked Michael.

'Come,' beckoned Charlie.

Michael approached and slotted himself in between a gap that opened between Huxley and Lynch. The former considered him with a smirk.

'Might want to put some ice on that,' said Huxley as he pointed to his own eye to indicate Michael's black one. 'Looks nasty.'

'I can see well enough to tell your nose still isn't straight,' retorted Michael.

In fact, much to Michael's annoyance, Huxley's nose had made remarkable progress in healing, but he knew that undermining the arrogant ass's narcissism was fertile ground.

'What is this, Charlie?' Michael probed again.

'Trouble,' replied the old man. 'House Littman looks to be on the warpath, or at least that's what it sounds like. Dominic, tell Michael what you told me.'

Charlie jabbed the cigar in Huxley's direction. A chunk of fresh ash fell from the tip and hit the desk.

'Some of my boys were doing their usual chores down the docks-' started Huxley.

Michael rolled his eyes.

'Damn it, Huxley, I thought we'd agreed on no more contraband,' he interrupted irritably. 'You know the cops are clamping down and we don't need the heat. What was it this time? Cocaine from Tetcheho, or stolen smartphones from Haikuza?'

'I may have been in the room when you said no more contraband, but I don't remember agreeing to it,' replied Huxley with a carefree shrug. 'I can understand you being a little confused, though, what with the pummelling your head took the other night.'

Michael stepped towards Huxley, his temper rising.

'You cocky, irresponsible son of a-'

'Enough!' barked Charlie. 'Keep it in the ring, you two. Dominic, finish your story.'

Huxley considered Michael through narrowed eyes as the latter retreated.

'So, as I was saying, the boys were running some errands, which always bag us a tidy profit I might add, when some of Littman's men bounced them and took the cargo. Now, given the price of coke these days, we're talking at least a million sovereigns here, not exactly spare change, so I ordered them to get it back. They tracked the Littmans to one of their dockside warehouses and persuaded them to return what was ours.'

'Let me guess, your version of persuasion involved broken bones,' said Michael dismissively. 'Please tell me no one got killed.'

Huxley tilted his head slightly and looked up at the ceiling, as if confessing to no more than stealing from the cookie jar.

'A few of them needed *strong* persuasion.'

Michael closed his eyes and pinched the bridge of his nose, exasperated.

'No wonder we're talking about a potential war. How can you be sure it was House Littman?'

'One of my guys recognised a few of theirs, plus the fact that our coke was in their warehouse. What more evidence do you want? Time-stamped written confessions?'

Michael looked to the head of the House.

'This could be bad, Charlie. We need to get ahead of it before it starts spiralling,' he said. 'No one needs a war.'

'True,' replied the old man, 'but according to Dominic it's all on Littman, not us.'

'Let me talk to him,' offered Michael. 'I wouldn't say we're best friends forever, but we worked out a truce on territory at the docks. I think there's some mutual respect there.'

Huxley stepped forward, his expression incredulous at Michael's suggestion.

'This is exactly the kind of weak pussying about that probably convinced Littman he could break this so-called truce in the first place. I say we gather the troops, march in, and take his territories. We send a message to that bald dirtbag, and whoever else is listening, that it's never a good idea to try your luck with the Trelanes.'

Charlie took a drag on his cigar and stared into space as he exhaled a long trail of smoke. Michael could tell he was mulling both options. After a moment, Charlie set the cigar down upon the gold ashtray and formed his fingers into a pyramid beneath his nose.

'Make the calls you need to, Michael,' he said.

'Wait, what?' blurted Huxley.

Charlie raised a hand to call for quiet.

'But I want Dominic coming with you as backup just in case things go bad. Littman's usually not one to make a play like this, especially over only a few packages of coke. Maybe it was just a rogue faction in his ranks. It that's the case, then we can work things out, no harm done.'

'I think killing some of his guys constitutes harm done, Charlie,' noted Michael dryly.

'Well, that'll be for you to help smooth over then, won't it? Besides, if they'd gone rogue, we did Littman a favour.'

'And if they weren't, his House's honour will make him demand something in return.'

'I'd rather pay blood money than real blood,' said Charlie. 'But we all know that playground rules don't apply. You try and make peace, but no one should be under any doubt that House Trelane is prepared for war.'

'That's the Charlie we've been missing,' said Huxley with a keen nod and a vicious grin.

Michael could tell there was no sense in debating any further. Charlie's mind had been made up. The old man retrieved his cigar and took another drag. His silence indicated the meeting was over. All the men bowed slightly and made for the exit, though Michael made sure he was at the end of the line. He waited for the last lieutenant to leave, then stopped and turned back to face Charlie. The head of the House glanced towards him.

'Anythin' else?' he asked gruffly.

'I saw Sarah, like you asked,' replied Michael.

'We'll deal with that later,' said Charlie to Michael's surprise. 'Go fix this Littman problem first, then we'll talk properly.'

Michael debated pressing on, as he knew the conversation would be just as difficult even if delayed, but he demurred. As keen as he was to get things off his chest, he recognised Charlie's logic that something so emotive was best left for quieter times and calmer minds, not ones preoccupied with a potentially looming gang war. It was House first and the personal second. Such priorities made sense to get to the top, but the cost was all too evident, as Michael himself had experienced at Sam's Coffee Emporium.

Michael nodded, retreated out the door, and closed it quietly behind him. He immediately started forming a plan, beginning with reaching out to Littman. He didn't exactly have the leaders of the other Houses on speed dial, but there were ways of getting messages to the right people. Michael was confident that enough respect existed between he and Littman from past dealings that House Trelane would at least receive a fair hearing. That was the hope anyway, as Michael had little appetite to take on responsibility of running the House while it was engaged in open warfare. Like the fight with Huxley, it felt like another test to prove his ability to lead, but this time employing brains rather than brawn. Michael hoped he wouldn't fail this one too.

6

POWER PLAYS

The Dominion Docks were as dark and dank as Michael remembered, whether from his first foray there as a boy, or the last time he had been close to the foul-smelling water almost a year before. They were the largest in the world and the most dangerous depending on your business and the hour of the day. The stink of graft, smuggling and criminality overpowered even the stench of the nightly fish markets and smoking dens in the part of the docks closest to the Gauntlet.

The vast hectares of rusting cranes and cargo containers obscured the huge vessels moored alongside. In some of the quieter, forgotten areas, homeless tramps huddled around burning oil drums, or desperate prostitutes positioned themselves strategically, hoping to entice off-duty sailors or bored dock workers. It was a cold, industrial nightmare that lacked any of the romanticism and colour the docks may have possessed during the age of sail, though even those illustrated images in the history books were no doubt distortions of the darker reality.

Michael stared out the car window, trying not to get too depressed by such thoughts, his mood already brought low by his meeting with Sarah. He averted his eyes as his vehicle drove past a painfully thin prostitute, who from the look of her had prioritised spending money on heroin rather than food or essentials. She smiled, revealing several gaps in her teeth, and exposed a wilted breast, somehow hoping that such a sight would prove enticing rather than pitiful.

Sarah had been right. Exploitation by the Houses was everywhere to see if you cared to look, but as Michael had just demonstrated by turning away, no one did care. Guilt briefly tugged at him, but he brushed it aside. The heroin, or any other poison the prostitute had become fixed on, could very well have been supplied by House Trelane, but it didn't matter. She had been responsible for her own fate and had made her own choices, just as

Michael had. Now she had to live with them, as did he. He felt no pity to offer.

Michael shook his head to drive away such dark thoughts and attempted to refocus. He couldn't help but feel a sense of déjà vu, as the small convoy of Trelane SUVs pulled up outside a huge warehouse belonging to House Littman. The previous occasion Michael had been there was to negotiate a deal with their head, Jonny Littman. While that House had no divine right to territory at the Dominion Docks, it was widely recognised that to directly challenge their presence was to court a fierce response. The potentially huge profits from extortion, corruption, and contraband was a prize they guarded jealously. However, that was not to say that House Littman was immune to reason, especially if there was potential benefit to its own self-interests.

House Trelane had access to various international crime syndicates and their wares that House Littman did not, whether cocaine or marijuana from the mountainous jungle regions of the Union of Tetcheho, or knock-off electronics copied from the high-tech industries of the Empire of Haikuza. It had taken Michael some time to sit and patiently negotiate face to face with Jonny Littman. The eventual deal allowed House Trelane to operate unmolested at the Dominion Docks in exchange for a percentage of the profits made going into Littman's coffers, but the loose partnership had been worth it for both sides. Until now it seemed.

After the war council in Charlie's study, Michael had spent hours trying to reach Littman, before finally the crime boss relented and returned his calls. He had been furious, of course, and issued the standard threats of preparing for war and vowing to crush House Trelane for such treachery and disrespect. Michael figured the theatrics were for the benefit of whatever audience was surrounding Littman at the time. From personal experience he knew the man to actually be quite calm, thoughtful and softly-spoken, if admittedly no-less dangerous for it.

After Michael had gone through the motions of showing suitable contrition, Littman had eventually agreed to a meeting to work out exactly what had happened and to see if a way forward was possible. Now, as the Trelane vehicles parked outside the warehouse that was widely recognised as the centre of Littman's dockland empire, Michael was keenly aware that his diplomatic skills were about to be put to the test. Never mind a resulting gang war, failure or a misstep in the coming minutes could mean Michael, Huxley, Lynch, and a dozen others wouldn't even make it out alive.

The driver stopped and switched the engine off. Huxley turned back from the front passenger seat and gazed wide-eyed at a contemplative Michael sitting in the rear.

'No pressure,' he said with a wink.

Michael ignored him and stepped out. He tugged the collar of his trench-coat slightly, guarding against the nighttime chill. He looked up at the old brown brick building, its surface stained with soot, with faded paintwork advertising previous occupants that had long since ceased trading. Michael advanced forwards and heard a series of car doors shut behind him and the sound of footsteps following. At least he wasn't walking into the lion's den alone.

As he approached the main entrance to the warehouse, the huge wooden doors swung open and several of Littman's foot soldiers emerged, each baring a sub-machine gun. For a fearful moment, Michael thought he and the others had walked straight into a trap, as it would take only a second for the guns to be pointed in their direction and unleashed.

'You Michael Ryan?' asked one of the men.

'I am,' replied Michael as calmly as his thundering heart allowed.

'The boss said we should bring you up to see him, so come on,' Littman's man continued.

'Hey wait,' interjected Huxley from somewhere behind Michael. 'He doesn't go anywhere without the rest of us.'

Michael somehow doubted the statement was made out of any concern for his wellbeing, and more to do with ensuring Huxley's interests were represented.

'The boss said just Ryan, nothing about you losers,' the henchman responded.

Michael glanced to the side as Huxley emerged into his field of view. He half-expected to see a gunfight erupt as Huxley's temper rose to the bait, so was surprised when the latter approached with his arms slightly raised.

'Look, how about it's just me that comes up with Ryan?' Huxley proposed. 'Here, you can even have my gun.'

Huxley slowly parted his trench-coat and made a deliberate show of plucking his semi-automatic pistol from its holster with his fingertips and handing it to the lead henchman, who examined it for a moment before pocketing it.

'I'll have to check with Jonny,' said the henchman, who turned away and started speaking quietly as he pressed a finger to his bluetooth earpiece.

Michael wasn't sure what to make of Huxley's uncharacteristically submissive display, but he wasn't convinced for a second it was genuine. The henchman turned and beckoned both men forward. As Michael stepped through the threshold of the warehouse, the henchman held out an open hand.

'Jonny says fine, but you need to hand in your piece as well, given how polite your friend here was.'

Michael sighed but offered up his own weapon without complaint. He'd never intended on its use, but it was better to have something to defend himself with in the worst case scenario. Now, the only thing he had in his arsenal was harsh language. For a fully-clothed man, he felt a strange sense of nakedness.

The lead henchman guided Michael and Huxley through a small maze of stacked wooden crates, with two other armed Littman thugs covering them from the rear. Eventually they reached a narrow rusted metal staircase that creaked as they ascended towards an office that overlooked the interior of the warehouse, as well as the parking area outside. The lead henchman opened the door, stepped aside and nodded for Michael to head through.

Michael stepped into the office and noted that the room hadn't changed since his last visit. For such a utilitarian warehouse clearly decades old, where one would have expected worn and dusty floorboards, peeling wall paint, and basic furniture, the inverse was true, bordering on garish. The wooden floor was smooth and varnished, the wall covered in dark pink paint and delicately lit by a central chandelier that generated an atmosphere more worthy of a boudoir than a working office. Thick red curtains were ready to be drawn across huge windows that looked out onto the docks. All the furniture was clearly designer, from the plush armchairs dotted around the room, to the conference table and chairs that dominated its centre, to the ornate marble and gold-leaf desk at the far end, behind which sat Jonny Littman.

Like the room, the man himself looked no different from last time. Tall and lean with sharp features, Littman wore an open-necked purple silk shirt and black leather trousers. His head was shaved smooth and a prominent scar ran down his left cheek, only slightly obscured by his neatly trimmed beard. A small diamond and ruby encrusted earring pinned to his right earlobe spelt J, while its partner on his left ear spelt L.

Littman rose from his own throne, equal in size to the one in Charlie's study but superior in jewel-encrusted opulence. He approached Michael, who held out a hand to shake. Instead of clasping it with his own, Littman reached into his trouser pocket and produced a small metal rectangular object. Before Michael registered what it was, Littman had already extended the flick knife and brought the tip of the blade to within an inch of Michael's eye.

'Tell me why I shouldn't blind you right here and now?' asked Littman calmly.

Michael resisted the overwhelming urge to jump back, hold his hands up in defence, or push Littman away.

'Well, the colour scheme here is so painful on the eyes, you'd probably be doing me a favour,' replied Michael coolly.

For a moment Littman unblinkingly stared. Michael breathed an internal sigh of relief as the crime boss's lips broke into a smile. He retracted the blade and pocketed it.

'Never one to mince words, Michael Ryan. I like that,' declared Littman. 'I was just joking anyway. If I take anything, it'll be your balls.'

Littman's smile vanished instantly and Michael was left under no illusion that the previous statement was nowhere near a joke. Littman turned towards Huxley, who had been quietly observing, and pointed.

'In fact, I should add this scumbag's tongue to the removal list. It was his men that killed mine, then stole my coke.'

'At least your payroll is lower this month,' said Huxley with a deliberate shrug, which only served to further enflame Littman. Michael quickly stepped in to cool things.

'That's what we're here to sort out, Jonny. House Trelane isn't looking for a war, we know how strong you are. I'm sure this was all just a big mistake, and one we'll put right.'

Littman's eyes narrowed as he considered Huxley, whose belligerent attitude was clearly not helping. The last thing Michael needed was a naked flame so close to the oil. He gestured towards the conference table.

'Let's talk this through,' he invited Littman.

The crime boss assumed his place at the head of the table. Huxley took the seat at the opposite end, while Michael sat in the middle, between the pair. He felt like a marriage counsellor.

'Firstly, House Trelane needs to apologise for any misunderstanding that led to this mess,' opened Michael. 'I know that-'

'No, we don't,' interrupted Huxley.

'Excuse me?' queried Littman, wondering whether he had genuinely heard such a brazen statement.

'We don't need to apologise for being superior to this dockyard trash,' continued Huxley with snide vigour. 'I just wanted to be here to tell him to his face.'

'What are you doing, Huxley?' asked Michael flatly, genuinely so flabbergasted he couldn't muster a suitably appalled tone.

'I do like that face, though. Cool scar. I'll make sure it's preserved when I mount your head on my wall.'

Littman's face had turned as pink as the walls. He slowly rose from his seat, his fists clenched white.

'You've just signed your own death warrant, Huxley,' he declared with cold fury.

'That's the spirit,' replied Huxley with a wink.

He formed the fingers of his right hand into the shape of a pistol and jerked it backwards, mimicking a gunshot. Michael just about registered the crack of glass behind him as a silenced sniper round pierced one of the office windows, entered Littman's right ear and exited through the left. With grim comedy, both of Littman's earrings were torn off and clattered onto the surface of the conference table, eventually resting near each other to spell JL.

The man himself remained upright for a moment before collapsing to the floor. The lead henchman looked around in panic before he too received a sniper round to the chest, immediately followed by the two remaining guards. As all three crumpled, Michael sprang up from his chair, in contrast to a relaxed Huxley who remained slouched in his.

'What have you done, you psycho?' whispered Michael in shock.

Huxley's eyes widened at the insult. To question his mental state was the ultimate slight. He once again formed his hand into a finger gun and aimed it at Michael. At first, Michael didn't feel the bullet hit him from behind, he just saw blood spatter across the conference table. A second later, it felt like a fire had been lit up inside his left shoulder. He instinctively clasped his right hand over the exit wound and cried out.

Michael didn't even have time to fully register the growing intensity of the pain before his right leg buckled as another sniper round tore into the thigh. Michael fell to the floor. He instinctively reached for his pistol holster only to find it empty, his weapon confiscated. Clever Huxley. Michael started to hear automatic gunfire in the interior of the warehouse. Michael guessed that with the hidden sniper having decapitated the leadership of House Littman, the rest of Huxley's men were pressing their assault with lethal brutality.

'Sorry to interrupt your peacemaker routine before it even got going,' said Huxley. 'But I was already bored with the charade, and as you can hear from outside, I don't have time to mess around. Consider it a hostile takeover.'

More out of desperation than hope, Michael pushed and pulled with his good leg and arm and started crawling along the floor towards one of the dead henchmen and the sub-machine gun he still held. He gradually found it easier to slide himself along the polished wooden floor, but given that it was his blood that made it so slick, that was not a good sign.

Michael was almost within reach of the weapon when Huxley, who had been watching the futile effort with amusement, rose from his chair and slowly ground his shoe down on Michael's outstretched hand. Michael groaned with pain, but refused to give Huxley the satisfaction of crying out, despite the ever increasing agony he felt in his shoulder and thigh. Instead he rolled onto his back and looked up at Huxley with as much hatred as he could muster.

'Damn you. Charlie will kill you for this,' he spat.

Huxley grinned wickedly.

'Not if I kill the old bastard first. Make no mistake, House Huxley was reborn tonight, but I need to get a lot more ducks in a row before I make a move on Charlie. And one of those ducks is having a little more fun with you.'

Huxley crouched down, pulled back a fist and slammed it with full force into Michael's face. The world went black.

7

THE SHROUDED MAN

Michael slowly stirred and instantly knew his nose was broken. The twin fires in his shoulder and thigh still smouldered. Notwithstanding having been knocked out, he felt lightheaded, no doubt from blood loss. He opened his eyes enough to glance at his shoulder and down to his thigh. He saw torn strips from what he guessed was his shirt wrapped tightly around the bullet wounds to form makeshift tourniquets. They were saturated with sticky, drying blood.

Michael attempted to move his arms and legs, but found them bound to the frame of the chair he had been placed on. He looked around the room and saw Huxley standing nearby, his arms folded as he checked his watch. Michael's nemesis had removed his trench coat and suit jacket, revealing rolled up shirt sleeves, as if he expected to get down and dirty into something. Not good. Meanwhile, Lynch sat on the conference table, slowly inserting new rounds into his silenced sniper rifle's magazine. He looked up briefly, met eyes with Michael and smiled wickedly.

'Nice work, if I say so myself,' he said.

Huxley cocked his head a little, as if considering a piece of art.

'True, but I think we can add a little more colour to the palette,' he said.

Huxley walked up to Michael, balled up his fist and right-hooked his seated victim. Michael momentarily saw stars and spat out a thick globule of blood.

'What's the matter, Huxley?' said Michael defiantly, blood discolouring his gritted teeth. 'Need me strapped down to make it a fair fight?'

'You know, that would sting if it had any credibility behind it,' retorted Huxley. 'We both know I owned you in that ring. If the old man hadn't called time, I would've broken you. Now I get to finish the job.'

'Spare me your crap, you've been wanting to do this for years.'

'Of course. But we can all get stuck in a rut and something needs to come along to shake us out of it. Mine was finding out that old fart was going to just hand you the House on a plate. Not only that, but he wanted you to take it legit. Well, fine, but something told me there wouldn't be a place for Sin and I in the brave new world of House Ryan.'

'The only places you belong are a padded cell for her and a sewer for you,' said Michael weakly, his words starting to slur a little.

He was in a bad way and knew it, but had no intention of going out with a whimper. His comment pressed Huxley's red button, as he knew it would. Huxley flew into a blind rage and started pummelling Michael with insane vigour. He was sure he felt at least a couple of ribs give way to the force and break. He groaned in pain, desperately trying not to give his assailants the satisfaction of hearing a scream. Eventually, Huxley eased off and shook his hands a little, grimacing as he extended and retracted sore fingers. Michael coughed up blood, another less-than-encouraging sign. Huxley turned to Lynch.

'Take over for a spell, will you?'

Lynch keenly hopped off the conference table with his sniper rifle. He stood in front of Michael for a moment, assessing the best part of the body to inflict pain on. He shrugged, spun the rifle around in his arms so that the shoulder-stock was directed at Michael, and smashed it down on the latter's stationary right hand. As multiple bones shattered, Michael could not stop himself from letting loose an agonised wail. When Lynch repeated the trick on his left hand, Michael cried out again, but this time less intensely. He had been prepared for the second strike that time, but also his energy was rapidly diminishing. He begged for the warm embrace of unconsciousness to escape the agony and despair for even a fleeting moment, but his body refused to comply, still wired as it was by pain and adrenaline. Michael felt the best he could do was distract Huxley and Lynch to gain at least some respite, no matter how short-lived, and getting Huxley to talk about himself would always guarantee a distraction.

'So how long have you been cooking this up for, Huxley?' probed Michael, his voice cracking.

Huxley looked at Lynch and nodded towards the office's exit.

'Make sure the boys have properly prepped the place and then light it up,' he ordered. 'I won't be long behind you.'

Lynch nodded and exited. Huxley stood for a quiet moment and gazed out the windows and to the docks beyond.

'Littman was right, we did attack first,' he said. 'There was no stolen cocaine. But I needed a reason to get you and him in a room together. The two of you negotiated last year, so it made sense Charlie would send Golden Boy Mikey on a peace mission, and just as predicable that you'd suggest one. You never did have the stomach for this business, always trying to wimp out and bring balance and order to things rather than just embrace the chaos. A clenched fist will always be more powerful than an open hand. Charlie used to appreciate that, but he's yesterday's man, a shadow of who he used to be. Even before Sarah left, he was going soft. If he'd had the sense, he'd have drowned Sin and I at the bottom of a lake, just like the rest of our House.'

'So you've been playing the long game?' asked Michael. 'Get me out of the way for you to become Charlie's number one, and manufacture a war with the Littman's to steer him back to how he used to be.'

'Until I'm done with him, at least,' acknowledged Huxley. 'By which time we'll have conquered all of Littman territory, grown Trelane power even more, and then I can step in to take over if…sorry, *when* Charlie succumbs to natural causes.' Huxley made air quotes with his fingers as he said the last two words. 'And after that, all hail House Huxley.'

Michael desperately wanted to leap out of his chair and throttle Huxley, or at least inflict enough damage to wipe the smug smile off his face before the end.

However, even without being tied down, Michael's body was a broken mess. He could barely keep his head up straight. Still, he was able to turn it towards the office's interior windows that looked out onto the warehouse floor. A yellow glow appeared and started to grow in intensity.

'That'll be the barbecue firing up,' observed Huxley.

He grabbed his jacket and trench-coat that were draped over a nearby chair and put them on, whistling cheerily as he did so.

'Well, it's been a pleasure, Mikey,' said Huxley as he slicked back his hair, his forehead already starting to moisten with the increasing heat. 'The last few minutes of torturing you, that is.'

Michael knew he was defeated. The injustice clawed at him, but he was determined not to go silently, even though he knew any words he had for Huxley would mean nothing.

'Walk away, but you'll always be the lesser man. You'll burn too one day, for what you've done. I'm just sorry I won't be there to see it.'

Huxley smirked, walked up to Michael and planted a foot on his chest. He shoved Michael backwards and he landed on the floor, hard. Pain cascaded throughout his body, from his broken ribs protesting against the force of Huxley's foot against them, to the re-ignition of searing fire at the entry wound to his shoulder. He wailed in agony. If Michael had been able to think straight and vocalise this thoughts, he was sure he would have called out for his mother, or for Sarah, no matter how pathetic it may have seemed to Huxley. The psychopath towered over Michael, his dark silhouette increasingly pronounced as the electric lights in the room shut off and he was bathed in the warm glow of the encroaching flames.

'Don't worry, I'll be sure to offer Sarah the comfort she needs, then show her what a good time a real man can offer her, not some street trash she once felt sorry for,' Huxley said spitefully.

He knelt down, grabbed Michael's hair and yanked his head up.

'What was it I said to you back at the fight? Oh yes, that was it.' He leaned in close to Michael's ear and whispered. 'Feel the burn.'

Huxley slammed Michael's head to the floor, stood and walked towards the exit, giggling maniacally as he went, no doubt amused at not just having the last word, but one infused with a certain vicious poetry. He opened the door and disappeared, but left it wide enough for Michael to see the flames licking at the door frame. Nearby, the interior windows began to crack and shatter with the heat. Whatever was in the hideous pink paint that covered the walls acted as an accelerant and the fire began to spread across the room and crawl along the ceiling. Michael, dazed from the blow to his head and already barely conscious from the universal pain and blood loss, could only look on with a sense of awe. The fire had an eerie beauty, like liquid sun.

Michael knew he was about to die. If the flames didn't reach him first, then the smoke or heat would do the job just as well, and perhaps more mercifully. He couldn't help but feel sorry for himself, but also angry. He raged at Huxley and Lynch, at the injustices they would get away with, and the fact that their takeover of House Trelane could not be stopped. Even worse was that Sarah was in Huxley's sights, and there was no telling what depravity the psychopath would visit upon her. Michael also felt angry with himself, not just for ending up the foolish victim of such an obvious power play, but also for the numerous opportunities he had squandered throughout his life. Most of all he felt angry that he wouldn't be able to say a proper goodbye to Sarah, to tell her how sorry he was for everything, that he had made a fatal error in choosing loyalty to a family that wasn't his rather than love and a life with her. It was too late for that, though. Michael would go to his grave absorbed by regret.

The flames had by now almost completely consumed the room. The chandelier dropped from its anchor and smashed onto the conference table. The plaster of the ceiling bubbled and dropped away, exposing the old wooden beams that had supported the structure for decades. They too started to char and buckle one by one, each collapse advancing closer to Michael as they buried all under them in flaming debris. He longed for the release that would be granted when the final beam gave way and smashed down upon him. There were only seconds left.

Then, Michael saw Death come for him. He had become well-read enough to have a passing knowledge of how the world's different cultures and mythologies personified the end of life. In Haikuza, it was a small black dragon that crawled down your throat and swallowed your soul before flying off. The Desert Kingdoms of Kartuush believed in a sprit made of sand that would form the faces of all your ancestors before adding your own spirit to its collection. As for the peoples of the Everlight Imperium, their interpretation was what Michael saw approaching him. It wore a black, flowing cloak that reached all the way to the floor, obscuring its feet. Not that it needed any, as it seemingly glided along the floor. A tattered hood shrouded the face in shadow. If mythology was any guide, had it been pulled back it would have revealed a skull with glowing eyes. They would be yellow for the sun, or red for fire. The colour would determine your destination in the afterlife, either spending it in the sunlit paradise of the Everlight Gardens, or enduring the ceaseless agony of burning for your sins in the eternal flames of Infernus.

As Michael considered the dark spectre approach him, he felt a growing terror that the hood would be pulled back to reveal red eyes. With the same clarity that he saw his life's mistakes and regrets, Michael realised that all the lies he had told himself over the years counted for nothing. They had been half-truths and exaggerations employed to fool himself into thinking that he was not really a bad man, let alone an evil one. He had just been doing his best to survive in a harsh world and what his mother had taught him, no matter how noble in intention, was not fit for the reality he found himself in. He may have had knowledge of evil deeds, but Michael was no Huxley, or Lynch, or even Charlie at his worst. They were the ones with ledgers filled with blood-red ink, not he, not Michael Ryan, who stood above it all while innocent people were abused and opponents murdered. But it was okay because he himself had no direct blood on his hands.

That was the lie. Michael could not even claim ignorance in defence. He had known of the evil, but went along with it, begrudgingly but not unwillingly. He was as drenched in blood as any of his cohorts. Sarah may have felt herself a hypocrite, but had at least been honest enough with herself to recognise it and, most importantly, possessed the courage to change her life. Now, as Death extended a claw-like hand towards

Michael's face, it was only as his life was about to be extinguished that he knew he was much worse than a hypocrite. He was a coward and would have no chance to redeem himself. As the spectre's hand covered his face and the flames around him were consumed by darkness, Michael Ryan knew that he was damned.

8

RESURRECTION

Michael slowly stirred, opening his eyes incrementally as if he were delicately parting a curtain to peek beyond it. Initially his vision was heavily blurred, revealing a collection of graduated blacks, greys and whites. The colours were clearly differentiated from each other, but they lacked form. He blinked a few times, hoping that the image would clear, but the world remained as if viewed through a smeared glass. Infernus was not what Michael had expected, but perhaps an eternity of blindness and confused senses was punishment enough, a never-ending limbo from which there would be no escape.

He gave up and closed his eyes. Michael attempted to listen instead. He heard a steady beeping in the background. It took him a moment to realise that it was the familiar sound of a heart monitor, as featured in numerous medical television dramas or soap operas.

Michael swallowed and groaned. It felt like a tiny gremlin had been rubbing his throat with sandpaper. He quickly realised just how parched he was, the kind of thirst that only a gallon of ice water could quench. As his mind cleared enough to grasp what his senses told him, Michael began to realise that rather than slowly roasting on a spit in the eternal flames, he was far more likely languishing on a bed in some kind of medical facility.

Michael managed to raise both arms, but with effort. He brought them up to his face and felt a gentle pull against his left forearm. His fingers probed around the area and he found the smooth plastic of a narrow tube that ended just under the coarse surface of a strip of surgical tape. It was an intravenous drip. That only added to the evidence that he was still alive and undergoing treatment.

Michael felt growing elation that he wasn't dead. The last thing he remembered was Death itself approaching, though he recognised that such a vision could just have easily, and more plausibly, been caused by blood loss or diminished oxygen to the brain. That terrifying experience felt like only minutes ago, interrupted by a brief period of dark, dreamless slumber. By some miracle it appeared that he had been rescued, and if only a few hours had passed, then there was still the possibility of getting a warning out to Charlie about Huxley's nefarious intent. Firstly, however, Michael needed to determine exactly where he was.

He used his right hand to rub his eyes and he repeatedly opened and closed them. Gradually his vision cleared and though the surrounding lights were dimmed to a comfortable level, Michael still squinted against them. It felt like he had emerged from a prolonged stay in an underground cave. How long had he been asleep? Even if it had been a few days rather than hours, there was still enough time to stop Huxley in his tracks and, more importantly, make a start on correcting the many mistakes Michael had made in life. Despite the confusion over his exact circumstances, the jubilation he felt at having a second chance easily eclipsed everything else.

After a few more blinks, Michael was able to take in his surroundings with clarity. Rather than the expected white, sterile environment of a typical hospital facility, he was baffled to find himself in something closer to a gothic castle or ancient temple. Dark grey stone walls, polished smooth, surrounded him. Lighter coloured cylindrical columns were placed at regular intervals and provided support for the ceiling above. Between the columns were intricately carved archways displaying various patterns along their arc. There were no windows of any kind, and so the only source of illumination emanated from lamps fixed to several columns and the ceiling.

Michael looked around his immediate vicinity and found himself surrounded by a range of medical equipment, including the IV bag that fed into his arm and the heart monitor that emitted the regular beep he heard. He was covered in a comfortable white cotton sheet, which he lifted with some effort. His arms felt weak and it was clear they had lost some muscle mass.

Michael saw that his lower half wore pyjama bottoms but that his upper torso was bare.

From it he could see that he had not just lost some weight, but a lot. His abdominals were still noticeable, but far less defined, as were his pectorals. While not emaciated, he looked like an athlete who had gone on a crash diet while neglecting to maintain his physique. Michael dropped the sheet and felt his face. Rather than pronounced stubble, his fingers embraced a fully grown beard. He reached for where the exit wound on his shoulder had been, only to feel the rough, discoloured skin of scar tissue. Panic began to gnaw at him that he had been out of things for more than just a few days.

Some movement in the shadows behind a nearby column caught Michael's eye and he saw a tall man with greying hair, beard and a kindly face emerge from behind it. The man wore smart trousers, a dark shirt and tie, and a white lab coat, which was fitting for at least some of the environment. He was studying several sheets of paper fixed to a clipboard as he walked, but froze as he looked up to see Michael staring at him. The doctor, or whatever he was, had clearly been expecting to see an unconscious patient, suggesting that such a sight had been the status quo for some time. It did little to assuage Michael's growing panic and confusion.

'Ah, you're awake,' said the doctor, reaching for something to say by stating the obvious.

The medic slipped the clipboard under his arm and approached Michael.

'Where am I?' Michael croaked, his throat as dry as desert.

The doctor stopped at the bedside and picked up a cup of water from a nearby side table, along with a straw. He placed the tip of the straw to Michael's lips and his patient drank greedily. The cool water felt as refreshing as a monsoon on a baked river bed, but was quickly withdrawn.

'Gently now,' said the doctor as he placed the cup back on the side table. 'I know your throat feels sore, but you'll have to drink little and often until you get used to it again.'

'Why does it feel this way?' whispered Michael, who discovered that a lower volume irritated his throat less.

'You had a respirator tube inserted for a while,' replied the doctor, who busied himself checking some of the systems that surrounded Michael's bed.

'For how long? What's going on? I want to know,' said Michael quietly but assertively. He was rapidly running out of patience, not that he had the energy to lash out physically.

'I think you'd better speak with your benefactor about that,' swerved the doctor.

He retreated to a nearby stone column and pressed a button on an intercom panel fixed to it.

'Felix, it's Kristian. Please ask Loman to come down to the infirmary and to bring some answers with him.'

'Who are you people? Who's Felix? Who's Loman?' demanded Michael, who couldn't help but raise his voice and instantly regretted it as he grimaced at the discomfort caused.

'This must seem strange and confusing, perhaps even a little frightening,' admitted the doctor. 'But please have a little patience and, well, at least some of your questions will be answered.'

Michael sighed loudly, making clear his frustration at not just being kept in the dark, but that he could do little but wait for the promised illumination.

'Answer me this at least,' he pleaded. 'How long have I been here?'

The doctor mulled a moment over whether to answer. Eventually he stepped forward to the bed, perhaps hoping being closer would provide some comfort. Michael could tell from the doctor's face it wouldn't be good news.

'I'm afraid there's no easy way to say it. You've been in a medically induced coma for three months.'

Michael scoffed in disbelief.

'That's not possible,' he insisted, shaking his head. 'I don't believe it.'

'Whether you choose to believe or not is irrelevant,' boomed a deep voice from the shadows just beyond the closest stone column. 'Not only is it possible, it is fact. But then three months to recover from death is not such a bad trade off, I would say.'

Michael used the support rails on the side of the bed to heave himself up, against the protests of his arms and torso. His ribs still ached, but the agony was nowhere near what he had endured in the burning Littman warehouse.

'What are you talking about?' he demanded, already slightly breathless from the exertion.

The owner of the voice stepped out of the shadows to reveal a tall and powerfully built man whom Michael guessed to be in his fifties. He wore black trousers and a long-sleeved turtleneck sweater of the same colour. His features were sharp, his face unsmiling and serious, his eyes dark and intense. A high hairline gave way to a stylish crew cut of pure white hair. The man continued to speak, his tone laced with a steely authority that commanded respect.

'You, Michael Ryan, died in the inferno you were pulled from,' said the mysterious man in black. 'For only a few minutes I grant you, but long enough to make it official. You would have remained so had it not been for this man.'

The man in black nodded towards the doctor, who remained stood to the side, his gaze shifting from the new entrant to Michael and back again.

'You're the one who pulled him from the flames,' said the doctor modesty.

'I was merely the delivery service. You brought him back from the dead,' said the man in black. 'My apologies, where are my manners. This is Doctor Kristian Mears, a consultant trauma surgeon at Dominion General when not lending us his time. He saved your life, which was no mean feat.'

'I've seen crash test dummies in better condition,' responded Mears as he sympathetically considered Michael. 'Truth be told it was touch and go. The extent of your blood loss, major internal and external injuries, plus smoke inhalation, all added up to a less-than-rosy picture. Once you were stabilised we had no choice but to put you in a coma to allow your body to heal.'

Michael tried to listen at the same time as his thoughts kept wandering in response to every new piece of information. As much as he did not want to accept it, the reality of his condition, from hair growth and weight loss to scar tissue and sore but healing bones, pointed to months having passed. He cast his mind back to the flames of the Littman warehouse and his last memories of that moment. The cloaked figure, the hooded face, the outstretched claw…

'That was you at the warehouse,' stated Michael as he turned his focus to the man in black. 'You were Death.'

'I prefer Gabriel Loman, if you don't mind. You may call me Loman. And nothing else.'

'Why save me?' pressed Michael.

'That is an answer which, by necessity, must wait until you are healthy enough to hear it,' responded Loman. 'Once you were taken off the respirator, we still thought it would be some time before you stirred. Evidently you have an impatient nature.'

'I feel fine,' snapped Michael. 'I want answers now.'

He swung his legs out from the bed, planted them on the cold stone floor and placed his full weight upon them. They instantly buckled and Michael collapsed to the floor, dragging his bedsheet with him. An unconcerned Loman folded his arms and raised an eyebrow.

'Thank you for proving my point,' he said, unimpressed.

Mears rushed over and helped Michael back onto the bed.

'Careful,' he insisted. 'Your wounds are well on the way towards healing thanks to enhanced treatments we gave you during your coma, but it'll take time to fully regain your strength.'

'So I'm a prisoner,' stated Michael as he adjusted himself on the bed with a groan.

'Of course not,' replied Loman. 'You're free to walk out at any time.'

He stepped to one side and used his arms to present a clear path that Michael could take if he so wished, but would find physically impossible to do so.

'You're a dick,' snarled Michael.

'I've been called worse,' the older man retorted, unperturbed.

'Give me time,' said Michael acidly.

'You have spirit, Michael Ryan,' replied Loman with a slight grin. 'I'm glad to see it also survived the flames. For what it's worth I appreciate your frustrations because I experienced them myself many years ago. As it was for me, most of the answers you seek will come soon enough. However, in the meantime, I offer this. Your being here has a purpose. You were not rescued by accident. We have been watching you for some time, gauging the right moment to offer a choice between damnation and salvation. Your enemies moved against you and provided that opportunity by ending your old life. You have, so to speak, been resurrected and a new life beckons. What you choose to do with it, we shall soon find out.'

It took Michael the rest of the day to accept that what Loman had revealed was the best information he was going to get. Of course, 'day' was a subjective term, with no available view of the sun's position, or any timepiece to indicate whether it was morning, afternoon or night. Despite Michael's protestations, Loman had walked away after delivering his cryptic message, as did Mears soon after, only briefly returning with a bottle of water and bowl of soup. Michael felt starved, but Mears insisted that he would need to be eased back into a normal diet, lest his stomach reject the solid food it had become unused to.

Having received what was clearly exemplary medical care, Michael reasoned there would be no sense in poisoning him. He quickly consumed his lonely meal and immediately tried to walk again, this time far more cautiously. He managed a few wobbly steps before his legs gave way, though he was prepared for it and used his arms to ease the fall. Frustrated but accepting of his situation, Michael sat on the cold, smooth stone floor and used his arms to push himself forward, along with what little strength he could muster in his legs to pull on his heels. He reminded himself of a dog dragging its backside across a carpet and couldn't help but chuckle, though there was nothing funny about the situation. Exhaustion was starting to make him feel almost drunk. Still, even with no possibility of walking out, he could make the best of it and explore his surroundings. Michael reasoned it would at least distract from his growing anxiety about his captors, as well as what fates had befallen House Trelane and especially Sarah during his time in unconscious limbo.

Disappointingly, Michael quickly discovered that his recovery area was the highlight of the room. As his eyes adjusted to the shadows beyond the reach of the nearby lamps, he spotted a heavy wooden door and dragged himself over to it. He was unsurprised to find that though the ancient iron handle turned, the door was locked. So much for not being a prisoner. Accepting defeat, and barely able to keep his eyes open, Michael crawled back to his bed and heaved himself onto it. Even though he felt too wired to sleep, within moments he had surrendered to it.

He dreamt of fire and heat and a shadowy figure reaching out for him. Michael woke in a cold sweat, momentarily overcome by the terrible thought that the burning warehouse was his reality and that Mears, Loman, and the stone infirmary were the unconscious respite. After a moment he settled and returned to fitful slumber. He did not dream of flames, but of Sarah, her back always to him, walking away and forever just out of reach no matter how hard he tried to keep up.

9

COVENANT

The days passed rapidly, especially after Mears had been kind enough to provide an old fashioned alarm clock with a large round face and two small bells atop it. It allowed Michael a sense of structure, of being able to tell how long he slept or how much time had passed between meals. He briefly considered smashing the clock and using a piece of the internal mechanism to pick the lock of the infirmary door, but quickly dismissed the idea. Despite the surreal nature of his confinement, Michael recognised he was not a slick operative in a spy movie. Besides, he had been provided with comfortable clothing and Mears would visit several times a day to check on his progress and provide nutritious food, so it was not as if Michael needed to escape from torturous captivity.

When he attempted to enquire about his situation, Mears would politely but firmly refuse to answer. His only response was that Loman would reveal all imminently. When Michael changed tack and queried why he had healed relatively quickly despite the seriousness of his injuries, Mears was more than willing to share, going on to talk passionately about advanced medical drugs that accelerated muscular and bone regeneration.

Michael barely understood the science, but was sufficiently curious to ask how Mears gained access to such treatments when, to his knowledge, no such revolutionary medicine was available at Dominion City's hospitals. For that matter, how could a leading surgeon be away from his post at Dominion General for so long, caring for a criminal brought back from the dead? Mears had merely smiled, a gesture that suited his warm demeanour, and suggested they continue building up Michael's walking strength.

After what he was sure had been a week, Michael was back on solid food, had become steady on his feet, and had even started to perform perfunctory push ups and ab crunches, to stave off boredom if nothing else. Michael picked himself off the floor after a particularly gruelling set which he knew he would regret later, and turned towards the infirmary door as he heard it unlock and open. He expected to see Mears, or 'Doc' as he had taken to calling him, walk through carrying a tray of food, but instead was confronted by Loman. He was dressed identically to the last time they had met and carried neatly folded clothing in one hand and a pair of clean running shoes in the other. He gently tossed them to Michael's feet.

'Are you ready for the answers you've been demanding?' Loman asked.

Michael picked up the clothes pile to find black jogging bottoms, socks and a hooded sweater.

'What is this? My regulation hour of outdoor exercise?' responded Michael bitterly.

'As I have told you, this is not a prison and you are not our prisoner,' said Loman. 'The infirmary door has been locked for your protection.'

Michael scoffed.

'Protection? From what? The truth about why I've been kept here while Sol knows what's happened to my House, to my friends, to-'

'Sarah?' Loman suggested.

Michael froze.

'How do you know about her?'

'I told you, Michael, we've been watching you. For quite some time in fact. There isn't much about you I *don't* know.'

Michael could only respond with a cold stare. He was desperate for answers but all he was getting was material for more questions. For days Michael had restrained himself from lashing out, from giving in to irrationality and baser instincts. He had resisted the call to rage and despair, hoping against hope that cooperation would somehow yield a better outcome. But his patience was now exhausted. It was a feeling he rarely experienced, and even on those occasions had left deep marks of shame and regret, but Michael knew he was one small spark away from erupting and unleashing uninhibited, murderous intent.

'Enough games, Loman. Give me the truth now, or weak muscles be damned, I *will* try and kill you where you stand.'

Loman's eyes narrowed slightly, though whether out of anger or in gauging the seriousness of the threat, Michael couldn't say. After a moment, he stepped aside and presented a clear path to the open infirmary doorway.

'After you.'

Michael followed Loman through the open portal and was disappointed to find a long stone corridor aesthetically similar to the infirmary, with a floor and walls of dark polished stone illuminated by regularly spaced lamps. He had imagined all kinds of scenes beyond the locked door, but nothing quite so pedestrian.

However, it added to his suspicions that wherever he was, it was unlikely to be above ground, as there were still no windows or natural light.

'Where are we?' he asked Loman as they advanced down the corridor. Michael kept a subtle distance behind, distrustful of being too close. 'And where's Mears?'

'This is the Citadel,' explained Loman. 'It is our base of operations beneath Dominion City. As for the good doctor, he can only get away with claiming pro bono work for so long.'

'So we *are* underground then,' said Michael, pleased with himself.

'Oh yes,' confirmed Loman. 'The core of the Citadel was likely built around the time of the Imperium's founding. By whom, we don't know. It was discovered about a century ago. These tunnels expand like a spider's web to most corners of the city, allowing us rapid access where needed. Indeed, there are unexplored areas even today that go deeper. We call them the Catacombs.'

Loman suddenly stopped and turned to face Michael. 'That is what I meant by protecting you. Had your door been left open, I've no doubt you would have attempted an escape. In fact, in any other situation, I would have welcomed such initiative. However, it has taken me years to gain familiarity with this place. You may have stumbled into the light through good fortune, but more likely would have become lost and found your way to a dark, lonely death. Given everything we have invested in you, such an outcome would have been... suboptimal.'

'Invested in me? You make it sound like I'm a recruitment prospect,' retorted Michael, far from impressed. 'And who is 'we'? I'm not deaf Loman. I've heard you use the plural several times, now and before. You said you had answers for me, so fess up.'

Loman stared a moment before tilting his head in the direction they had been walking. They carried on, though Michael was sure the pace had increased. It was plausible that Loman was as keen to reveal what was going on just as Michael was to hear it.

'You are not wrong,' said Loman as they walked, his hands clasped behind his back. 'You *are* a recruitment prospect and have been for longer than you realise. 'We' are the Covenant, a secret organisation founded a century ago. Our mission is to stand for justice in an all-too-unjust world, to defend the weak and helpless from those who would seek to exploit and crush them, and to protect Dominion City from that which would harm or even destroy it.' Once again Loman paused, turned and stared intently at Michael. 'In short, we exist to stop people like you.'

Michael was so surprised by Loman's words that he took a step back without realising it, as if the man had physically jabbed him with an accusatory finger rather than cutting language. He swallowed hard and struggled to form an appropriate response. Michael was apparently being considered for an organisation that existed to combat men such as him. What response was appropriate, given the confusion such a prospect generated? In the end, Michael let his gut answer for him, influenced by the defiance he felt at his recent treatment.

'Well, you haven't been doing a very good job for a very long time,' he responded coldly.

Loman let out a sigh and looked up to the arched ceiling of the corridor.

'You are not wrong about that, either,' admitted the older man. 'For too long we have existed in the shadows. I am as guilty as any of advocating such a course. But now I believe a new one is required, one that combines the best of my predecessors.'

Michael suddenly realised they had stopped at a junction in the corridor. Down a short passage he could make out what looked to be a huge chamber. The light inside was far softer than the blunt fluorescents that illuminated the corridor. Loman beckoned Michael to follow him through.

'Come. Time to meet those predecessors,' he said. 'Welcome to the Shrine.'

Michael followed and was stunned to find the passage led into a circular chamber as large and ornate as any solar temple. Instead of the stonework of the rest of the Citadel, there was black marble throughout. The walls and columns reached up over a hundred feet to a ceiling concealed by darkness. Carvings of gargoyles, human skeleton figurines, and mythological creatures clung to the sides of the columns, looking down as if they had been watching some forbidden ceremony long ago and were frozen in place for the blasphemy of daring to observe.

The inky blackness of the ceiling was disrupted by an ornate glass dome, the supporting framework of which looked to be made of silver. From the dome emanated a soft white light which bathed the chamber and gave the whole space an eerie, ethereal quality. Michael felt as if he had stepped out of reality and entered a world of the dead.

At the centre of the chamber was a raised solid circular platform about ten feet high. A short stairway spiralled upwards to allow access to the top. As Loman ascended the steps, Michael was careful not to trip on them as his attention was dominated by the surroundings. It took only a moment to reach the top, whereupon he was taken aback to be confronted by six figures. Each stood upon a plinth and were regularly spaced around the edge of the platform to complete a circle of their own. Michael hadn't noticed it before as his eyes adjusted to the new environment, but six subtle shafts of light came down from the dome above to illuminate each figure.

Michael quickly realised they were motionless statues or mannequins. Each wore a different combination of clothing and body armour and there was clear progression in the level of technology apparent in each outfit, from a basic if beautifully sculpted metal chest plate, to sections of modern kevlar body armour. Michael paused his examination of the last outfit. It looked like the shrouded figure that had pulled him from the flames at the Littman warehouse, only now he was able to get a far clearer view of it.

The long, black flowing cloak was as he remembered, its base and sleeves ragged and torn, evoking decay, as if it had just emerged from the grave. The large cowl still obscured the face, but Michael leaned in closer and within the shadow of the hood found a mask of black fabric that covered the whole head except for two discs of reddened glass that formed some kind of goggles. The main outfit was a svelte battle suit of fabric, leather and armour plating, all black. At the centre of the belt was a buckle on which was carved a symbol; two rings adjacent to each other, a black line pointing in a southwest direction emanating from the right ring, an identical black line pointing northeast from the left one. Where hands should have been were dark metal gauntlets with sharpened edges and talon-like fingers. They had been the nightmare claws reaching out to Michael through the fire. He turned to Loman, who had been waiting patiently.

'Very theatrical, but why dress up like a monster?' he asked.

'I am the most recent link in a chain that stretches back over a hundred years,' said Loman. 'Just over a century ago the first of us, the founder of the Covenant, rose from the ashes of the death almost all had assigned to him. In doing so he found both his purpose and the name of the champion the Covenant would employ for its cause. You are in the company of the Wraiths.'

Mounted a few feet to the right of Loman's outfit was one that looked almost a century old. A long, flowing dark grey greatcoat was complimented by a black leather battle suit, polished cavalry riding boots, metal wrist guards and leather gloves with studded knuckles. A cowl identical in colour to the coat concealed an iron mask with suitable slits for the mouth and nose and rectangular reddened glass eyes. An ornate breast plate dominated the upper torso, at the centre of which was a symbol, this time of an arrow pointing northeast, at the base of which was a cross with a dot either side. It reminded Michael of a sword and hilt. He looked down when he felt a slight elevation under one of his running shoes.

Underneath his toes was a bronze plaque. The words IRON-WRAITH were engraved on it. Curious, Michael moved to each of the other figures in a clockwise direction, as it was clear he was moving forward in time based on advancements in each battle suit's style and technology. In order, the four plaques after Iron-Wraith read PHOENIX-WRAITH, STEEL-WRAITH, TITANIUM-WRAITH and NIGHT-WRAITH. Michael ended up back in front of Loman's battle suit and looked down. The plaque read SHADOW-WRAITH.

'Wraiths?' queried Michael in response to the plaques and Loman's declaration.

'A wraith is a spectre, a spirit, a phantom,' explained Loman.

'I know what a wraith is,' retorted Michael impatiently. 'But why call yourselves that?'

'Because all of us were or are one,' replied Loman. 'Each Wraith who has served was brought back from physical or spiritual death in some way. The name was chosen to represent something beyond life and death, something elemental, a manifestation of justice or punishment depending on the eye of the beholder.'

Loman stepped over to Iron-Wraith's battle suit and gazed at it reverently.

'To the public, Iron-Wraith was known as Lord Conrad Steel, by his own admission a vain and arrogant nobleman who had only known luxury and hedonism throughout his youth. There was no doubting his bravery, however, and upon commencement of the great war between the Imperium and Kreigvoss, he served as an officer on the frontlines. If the bloodshed he witnessed did not change him, then capture and the experience of a Kreigvossian prisoner of war camp surely did. He eventually escaped and found himself in the Realm of the Shadow Peaks, to the south of Kreigvoss. It was then as it remains today, a cold, barren, mountainous and mysterious place, its secrets all too impenetrable. After several years, Conrad reappeared in Dominion City, a changed man determined to bring some semblance of balance to a corrupt and chaotic order. He formed the Covenant, so named for the promise made to society, the oath of protection that I spoke of earlier, the same one we strive to uphold today.'

Michael slowly took in each of the other battle suits as Loman spoke. Phoenix-Wraith's was more a quiet evolution of his predecessor's garb, with greater hints of colour, especially red, yellow and orange, as well as updated gear such as combat boots and armoured knee and elbow pads.

However, Steel and Titanium-Wraiths were, in Michael's estimation, trying far too hard. Steel-Wraith had clearly sought to pay homage to the iron original, but had markedly ramped up the amount of metallic armour plating in his battle suit. Titanium-Wraith had gone all-in and had sacrificed any subtlety in favour of resembling a sleek battle tank on legs.

The suit that followed belonged to Night-Wraith. It could not have been more different from its metallic cousins. Entirely black, it was difficult to make out even under the shaft of light, but had ditched all grandiosity, power and protection in favour of stealth and minimalism. Its cowl and mask may have been consistent with past iterations, but the coat or cloak had been dropped in favour of tight-fitting fabrics and armour plating shaped to the contours of the body. Michael was reminded of a Haikuzan ninja.

As he scanned each suit, Michael checked for symbols. Phoenix-Wraith was marked by a triangle which contained a small version of Iron-Wraith's sword-like symbol. Steel-Wraith's was identical to the one belonging to the Covenant's founder, except the sword had two hilts, while Titanium-Wraith had three, as if each successor Wraith felt that he was somehow levelling up. Night-Wraith, as with his battle suit, had broken from tradition and adopted a new symbol, a single ring and southwestern-pointed line. Loman's Shadow-Wraith symbol had added an additional ring and line, as if he were the next evolution from his own predecessor.

'I get the change of outfits over time,' said Michael. 'But why the symbols?'

'They are alchemical in origin,' answered Loman. 'Iron for Iron-Wraith, obviously. Phoenix-Wraith combined that symbol with the one for fire, a triangle. Steel and Titanium-Wraith's preferred to feel like true successor's to Conrad, and so re-adopted his symbol but added small additions. Night-Wraith, my own recruiter and mentor, felt the Wraiths had become too much like blunt instruments and that we would do better to operate from the shadows, striking in the dark and instilling fear and superstition in the criminal fraternity. His symbol represents night. When he passed the mantle on to me, I agreed with his thinking, but believed that we should aim to keep our oath at all times. Therefore, my symbol represents night but also day, when shadows can exist in all places at the right moment.'

'Every day's a school day,' retorted Michael. 'But everything you've told me doesn't even begin to scratch the surface of the questions I have.'

'No doubt,' Loman remarked. 'Nevertheless, that's all you're going to get for now. Whether you hear the rest, or none at all, depends on the choice you make next.'

'What choice?' demanded Michael. 'To become a Wraith, like you?

'Frankly yes, if you want it,' replied Loman bluntly. 'My usefulness to the cause is reaching its end. Too many war wounds. New blood is needed. The next Wraith must take his place alongside our past champions.'

Having been prepared for obfuscation, Michael was at a loss for words at Loman's honesty.

'Don't look so surprised,' the man behind Shadow-Wraith said. 'The Covenant recruits the Wraiths from the fallen of humanity, oftentimes criminals such as yourself. We do so because having walked in the shoes of the enemy, you are better equipped to understand them, to appreciate their motivations and mindsets, to recognise strengths and exploit weaknesses.'

'Providing these prospects even want to join,' said Michael sardonically.

'Indeed,' admitted Loman. 'But that is why our candidates are carefully monitored and selected, to determine if they would be open to at least the possibility of beginning a new life, or whether they are so subsumed by their dark existence that they can never countenance any form of release from it. Ultimately, how much do they desire redemption for sins past, and if they do, are they even worthy? *That* is the choice you face, Michael Ryan. Be honest, did you ever truly feel comfortable with the life you were leading, absent of any regret and free of remorse? I looked into your eyes that night as the flames lapped at your feet. The terror in them as I reached out could only be borne by a soul that knew it was destined for a dark place. You died and were resurrected, an appointment with the afterlife postponed long enough to bring balance to your life's ledger, should you so wish. Second chances are rarely gifted and all too often squandered.'

Michael looked away, unable to meet Loman's piercing gaze.

'The coming hours will determine what you do with that chance,' said the older man as he pulled out a small pistol from his pocket, aimed it at a shocked Michael and pulled the trigger.

With a tiny whoosh, a small dart hit Michael's neck, finding the carotid artery. The volume of tranquilliser was small, but was so potent that Michael barely had time to reach for the dart before his eyes rolled back into his head and he crumpled to the floor. Loman pocketed the pistol and breathed deeply.

'I hope to Sol I'm right about you,' he said as he considered the unconscious Michael. 'We-' he paused and checked himself. '*I* can't afford a repeat of last time. No one can.'

He turned around and stepped over to the outfit belonging to Shadow-Wraith and gently laid a hand on its chest. Loman closed his eyes, trying and failing to deflect a painful memory.

'Forgive me, but I have to take this chance, for his sake, for mine… and for hers.'

10

MEAN STREETS

Michael awoke with a start and instantly reached for his neck. He felt nothing. As the mental fog gradually lifted he took in his nighttime surroundings. Still dressed in the clothing Loman had provided, Michael found himself under a grimy blanket. Several layers of flattened cardboard boxes acted as a makeshift mattress beneath him. He felt a continuous draft of warm air against his back. Michael turned over to find himself next to a heating vent. It was a trusted method he employed as a youth to keep from freezing to death while sleeping on the streets.

Many of those streets looked exactly like the one he had awakened in, a narrow alleyway filled with dumpsters, discarded bottles, loose papers and rags. Half a dozen other homeless were scattered about, copying his method of staying warm. A line of wall lamps and their harsh yellow light were only mildly successful in penetrating the gloom. Michael instinctively knew where he was and greeted the realisation with a lurch in his stomach. He was back in the Gauntlet.

He did not even need to flashback to his youth. Barring bodily changes, Michael could have swapped places with the cynical and distrustful boy of twelve years previously, who presented a stoic facade but would combat anxiety every night as he tried to drift off to sleep. There was the constant fear of having his backpack and its precious contents stolen while he slept, what morsels of food he had squirrelled away being raided, or in the worst case his young body being violated. As well as antagonising too many of the wrong people through his own thievery, it had been the near-constant fear that drove Michael out of the Gauntlet.

Now, as his confusion cleared, there was no fear, only anger. There was the immediate anger at being dumped in a bad memory, his promise to never again set foot in the cursed place broken through no choice of his own. There was anger directed at Loman and the strange

Covenant organisation over his treatment, regardless of their self-professed redemptive motivations. Above all, Michael's anger was focused on Huxley. Not just anger, but rage. It burned within him with all of the ferocity of the flames which had claimed the Littman warehouse and almost consumed him as well. What were the last words Huxley had whispered bitterly into Michael's ear? *Feel the burn.* Well, he felt it all right, and promised himself he would make Huxley feel it too.

Michael flung aside the soiled blanket, picked himself up and headed with determination towards the end of the alleyway. He needed to reach the Trelane estate as quickly as he could and get his life back in order. He may have been absent for three months, and though his tales of underground fortresses and secret societies would almost certainly appear farfetched to Charlie, what couldn't be so easily dismissed were the faded scars where Lynch's bullets had left their mark. He had no evidence of Huxley's ultimate plan to take control of the House, but then Michael's word was usually all the old man required. He would set the world to rights, but first he needed money and transport.

Michael emerged from the alley and was depressed, if not surprised, to find the Gauntlet an even more miserable place since his departure. There was a nightlife, even a vibrant one, if not of a wholesome kind. Many side streets were drab and dank, dominated by crumbling apartment blocks with their graffiti-strewn walls and broken or poorly functioning street lighting.

However, the main drag of the Gauntlet was awash with sickly neons and garish advertising boards. Most of the businesses were low-grade, be they pawn shops, gambling dens, strip clubs and dive bars. Defended by barbed wire, there were convenience stores, steak houses, fried chicken restaurants and hotdog stands, along with a range of other options for a quick snack or pack of cigarettes. Even pimps, hustlers and gangsters needed a break while not exploiting the citizenry.

The street bustled with people and reflected a mix of social strata, from homeless beggars and drug addicts to suited stockbrokers from the Golden Gateway in search of consequence-free debauchery. In between were ordinary people trying to scrape by on an honest living, be they dockworkers, sweatshop seamstresses, or a multitude of other jobs, none of which paid enough to afford an escape from the Gauntlet, but at least avoided homelessness. Michael briefly flashed back to his mother and how she tried to make their tiny apartment an oasis of escapism amidst the desperation. It had only been when she vanished that he was forced onto the streets, and the reality of the Gauntlet after dark was exposed to him.

He shook away the memory, not wanting to think about his mother and the pain of his early years. However, some experiences, if not thought of fondly, were at least valuable to his current predicament. Michael needed money to get across town, and just as the crowds in front of him had provided a buffet of options in his youth, so did they now. With his hoodie concealing his face, Michael casually leaned back against a wall, on the lookout for a suitable target.

It had taken him many painful lessons to perfect the art of pickpocketing. His earlier stumbling efforts had often resulted in beatings from the prospective victim for the audacity of making an attempt. Eventually, though, Michael perfected the formula, and his ill-gotten gains were often the only thing that stood between him and starvation. He found the trick lay in selecting the right person. There was little point in stealing from those at his level. Even if they had anything, which was rare, Michael's moral compass in his youth had always insisted on punching upwards and not exploiting downwards. He was bitterly aware of the contradiction the past twelve years represented in that regard, but, like memories of his mother, he shrugged away such thoughts.

The prowling businessmen in their thousand-sovereign suits were the optimal target for those new to the game, but Michael knew better. While some were naïve, most knew the perils of the Gauntlet and were careful to avoid bringing expensive phones, watches or jewellery. They only carried cash because it was all that was needed to have a good time and avoid illicit purchases appearing on credit card statements. Even if said cash wasn't kept in secure money belts, such affluent groups, especially the more experienced tourists, hired tough and streetwise bodyguards to look out for potential threats. They would see Michael coming a mile away.

That left the middle layer of the cake, either the average working person or the social parasites of the Gauntlet who lorded it over their patch, be they pimps, loan sharks, drug dealers and the like. Suddenly feeling an intense desire to somehow punish his old neighbourhood, even in an abstract sense, Michael knew which target he preferred.

He slowly scanned his surroundings, but it did not take long to find a repellant spectacle. Close to the mouth of a nearby alley, a flamboyantly dressed pimp was lecturing a sorrowful-looking young prostitute in the middle distance. The pimp was at least a foot taller than the girl and used his height and bulk to lord over her. His long velvet coat and soft cap kept him warm while the girl tried to suppress shivers as her scanty clothing did little to protect against the nighttime chill. Michael set off slowly at first to judge the right moment. It came as the pimp screamed at the terrified girl, who visibly shrank at the verbal assault. Michael was too focused on his approach to pay full attention to the cause of the pimp's wrath, but it had something to do with the girl being reluctant to satisfy a particular client's troubling fetishes. In any case, the pimp's emotions would cloud his awareness of his surroundings. A few feet away, Michael deliberately feigned drunkenness, his walk unsteady, his speech slurred. He clumsily bumped into the pimp.

'Spare a crown, please, chief?' Michael pleaded pathetically, though he suspected a quarter of a sovereign would still be too much. He followed up with a dry heave. As hoped, the pimp shoved Michael away, keen to get rid of the wreck of a man.

'Get out of here, street scum!' he thundered.

Michael dismissively waved a hand at the pimp and cursed. With his other hand, he discreetly deposited the stolen wallet into the pouch of his hoodie and carried on stumbling away. He slowed as he heard the young prostitute scream and glanced back to see the pimp pin her arm behind her back and twist it at an unnatural angle. It was a punishment designed to inflict severe pain without leaving any bruising. Clients wouldn't pay as much for less appealing products.

For a moment, Michael considered stopping. The young girl's cries for mercy pierced through the white noise of street life, whether the hustle and bustle of the crowds, the honking of vehicles, or the thumping music emanating from dive bars and strip clubs. Like the sound of a crying child, her pleas stirred a primal feeling in Michael. He suddenly heard his mother's voice, as clear as if she were standing next to him. *If you can't find the good in the world, you should be it.*

Michael felt the urge to turn and rush to the girl's defence. He had to admit that some of Loman's words had landed with him. Combined with his regrets as the warehouse flames crept nearer, there was an acknowledgement that life simply couldn't carry on as before. Nevertheless, it was foolish to think that he could just turn from being a career criminal into some shining defender of justice. He would make positive changes, but within the life he knew.

Michael kept walking, then broke into a run and rounded a corner into a side alley, at the end of which was a high brick wall. It didn't matter, as Michael tapped into the muscle memory of his parkour days and the teenage stray inhabited the grown man. He used a crate to leap to a taller dumpster and, in turn, used that to launch himself towards the half-descended ladder of a fire escape. Michael grabbed the bottom rung and used the ones above it to pull himself up to a grilled platform.

Without pausing, he bolted towards the wall of the adjacent building, jumped, pivoted at just the right angle, and used the momentum and grip of his running shoes to find purchase on the brickwork. Michael managed a couple of steps before gravity exerted itself. He boosted himself off the wall just before falling to the damp, rubbish-strewn street.

Michael soared through the air for less than a second, grabbed the top of the wall that sealed off the alley and hauled himself up. He crouched upon it and rechecked his surroundings. The fierce pumping of his heart drew his focus, the screams of the young prostitute relegated to fading background noise. Michael's conscience may have tugged at him, but he needed to prioritise. Getting back to the Trelane estate and reclaiming his life was all that mattered. He peered over the wall and saw a collection of garbage bags piled on the other side, ideal to cushion a fall. He flung himself off and dropped fast, glad to be putting the Gauntlet behind him once again and forever.

11

THE NEW PRINCE

With a decent handful of sovereigns at his disposal, Michael needed only a few hours to reach Green Acres, first by the city's grimy metro system and then by taxi. He made sure to be dropped off down the road from the Trelane estate to have time to scout the perimeter. Caution was the watchword. If Huxley or any of his minions spotted Michael before he could reach Charlie, he would doubtless catch a bullet to the head before uttering a word.

In the same way Michael's brief reunion with the Gauntlet had caused unpleasant memories to resurface, so did the stealthy approach towards the estate. After over a decade of exploring the mansion and its grounds, what had been a curiosity back then was now so clear in Michael's mind that he could have navigated them blindfolded. He quickly located the tree used to scale the wall and swiftly climbed it. He had to admit that whatever drugs Doc Mears had been pumping him with had indeed worked miracles. As with his impromptu parkour display back at the Gauntlet, nimble agility came effortlessly. He felt only slight fatigue despite the late hour. There remained some tenderness in the muscles and bones Huxley and Lynch had so effectively brutalised. Still, under normal circumstances without wonder drugs, Michael reckoned they would have been only half-healed with months of physiotherapy to look forward to.

He perched upon the large branch that had once been the gateway from his old world to a new one. Michael had not known what to expect upon arriving, but it certainly hadn't been a party. Instead of a vast outdoor celebration as with Charlie's birthday, he spotted several dozen guests in tuxedos and ballgowns congregating on the veranda just outside the ballroom at the mansion's rear, clinking cocktail glasses or puffing on thick cigars. Though he couldn't see clearly through the open doors and large glass windows of the ballroom itself, Michael assumed there were hundreds more guests inside based on the movement of bodies and sounds of assorted chatter and cheers. He racked his brain for why such an event was happening but couldn't settle on one. Michael was unaware of any family birthdays, national celebrations or House occasions that fell during spring. Still, if there was a party of that size going on, Charlie would surely be hosting, meaning an opportunity would eventually present itself for a discreet reunion.

The thought that Huxley may have used the previous three months to make his move briefly crossed Michael's mind, but he dismissed it. Huxley had a growing power base, but he would need a critical mass before attempting to take the throne without sparking a civil war or risking the other Houses striking during the upheaval. Such a strategy would take time. Between war with House Littman and questions over his disappearance after the fire, Michael expected Charlie to be wise enough not to take his hands off the wheel in favour of Huxley, whatever his previous intentions for retirement. Michael briefly wondered how his nemesis had explained away the events of the warehouse. No matter, he would ask Charlie himself once Huxley's treachery was exposed. The hour was getting late, but with any luck, the party, whatever its original purpose, would become a welcome home celebration for Michael and a wake for Huxley. But first, he wanted a closer look at the event itself.

Michael dropped down from the branch, hit the ground and rolled. He made swift progress through the estate grounds, ducking, sliding and crawling where needed to slip past the guard patrols. He made judicious use of hedgerows, walls and ornate garden sculptures to conceal himself from the panning eyes of the numerous security cameras, which, like the estate grounds, he was all too familiar with. Michael knew better than to approach too close to the ballroom, so he made his way to the side of the mansion, where it was quiet. He ran up to the wall and used the copious ivy and vines that grew across the brickwork to ascend several floors. He hauled himself onto a balcony and then leapt to an adjacent one. Michael repeated the process several times until he had rounded the rear corner of the mansion and found himself close to the ballroom. Several dozen feet below, the party guests enjoyed the night air. They continued chatting and drinking, oblivious to the uninvited stranger observing them.

A line of bricks jutted out from the wall between the balcony Michael found himself on and another several metres away. He stepped out and found enough space to get a toe-hold with both feet. Michael dropped down but caught the bricks with his fingers, bracing his feet against the wall below. He shimmied to the right and maintained his position as if taking a short break during free-climbing a coastal cliff. It was not exactly comfortable but had the benefit of allowing him a decent view of the ballroom through a ventilation grate. The warm lighting cast by the chandeliers complemented the polished mahogany of the floor and walls. A string quartet tucked in the corner of the room provided musical accompaniment.

Michael scanned the crowd and quickly locked in on Charlie. He wore a sharp tuxedo and held a smouldering cigar, which he waved around like a wand while relaying an anecdote from the glory days. It didn't take long for Michael to spot Huxley holding court in front of a group of sycophantic admirers. Sinderella hung on his arm like a mascot, daring the men in the group to admire her low cut dress while pretending to listen to her brother. Lynch skulked nearby and briefly turned away to discreetly snort something from the tip of his thumb. Michael was surprised to see drugs being taken so openly when a generally conservative Charlie had often come down hard on such things. In his estimation, it was one thing to sell them for profit, quite another for his men to indulge themselves. The fact that Lynch hadn't retreated to the bathroom to get his fix indicated confidence that Charlie and his values wouldn't be a hindrance for much longer.

Michael's attention, along with the rest of the guests inside the ballroom and those on the veranda, was grabbed by the high-pitched clinking of metal on glass. He spotted Charlie tapping a champagne flute with a spoon and the crowd duly quietened.

'I'd like to thank you for comin' tonight,' the host began. 'Even if my catering budget doesn't.'

The guests laughed on cue. Michael rolled his eyes at a line of humour that Charlie clung onto way past signs of life.

'But in times of triumph, why not enjoy ourselves?' asked Charlie rhetorically. 'Victory shouldn't be celebrated quietly, but loudly and proudly, and friends, House Trelane is truly victorious!'

The statement was met with a roaring cheer and raised glasses. Michael could only think Charlie was referring to conflict with House Littman. After the attack at the warehouse, it would have been the only outcome, especially after Littman's murder. No House could tolerate the death of its master, whatever the consequences of going to war. From the look of things, they had placed honour first, rolled the dice, and been destroyed for taking the gamble.

'As we speak, the Littman's are either dead, on the run, or in our hands,' declared Charlie with a hint of steel in his tone. 'Their territories are now ours, their treasury adds to our own, and as their light is snuffed out, ours only burns brighter.'

Michael had to hand it to his mentor. Charlie had a gift for knowing just what to say to rally the troops. The old man slowly advanced through the crowd as he spoke. Michael suddenly saw that the master of House Trelane was heading towards Huxley, who awaited appreciatively. The guests between the two men cleared a space as Charlie approached his young enforcer.

'No House owes all to one man, just as one man can't expect a House to owe him everythin'. But this I can say.' Charlie stood in front of Huxley and placed a firm hand on his shoulder. 'Without Dominic bringin' his energy, drive, and loyalty to our flag, makin' the hard choices, and doin' what it takes to win, we wouldn't be celebratin' tonight. If you honour me, you honour him.'

Michael's stomach lurched at seeing Charlie look upon Huxley with the admiration of a proud father considering a favoured son. At that moment, all became clear. Despite Charlie's warm words about loyalty, there was none in House Trelane. Even if the old man had merely been stroking Huxley's ego and quietly recognised the danger the young prince posed, it didn't matter. Like Michael before him, Huxley was just a pawn for Charlie to move around the game board as the situation required. There hadn't been one word uttered during Charlie's speech about Michael or any other fallen soldier. He had already been forgotten, just another expendable piece.

Michael had measured up when it suited Charlie to entrust his empire to someone he could rely on not to kill him five minutes into retirement. Now, having faced a war, even one forced upon him, Charlie had no reservations in releasing his attack dog Huxley and, in doing so, helping to burnish the fading status of House Trelane. He certainly didn't look like a man tired of life and verging on retirement. Maybe the hunger had returned, the insatiable desire to accumulate power that was as much a drug to Charlie as whatever powder Lynch was snorting. Perhaps Charlie would do away with Huxley when the time was right, and the psychopath no longer suited his purposes, but Michael wouldn't be there to see it.

The scales had fallen from his eyes, and the regrets he felt as Loman reached for him through the warehouse flames came flooding back. Michael had truly wasted his life in service to nothing. After attempting to bury such thoughts after waking up back in the Gauntlet, he instinctively sought to return to his comfort zone, to forget about the hard questions he had started to ask himself and that Loman only emphasised. But now, there was no warmth, no comfort zone, no return. There was just cold loneliness.

Michael looked away, unable to bear the sight of his would-be executioner being embraced by Charlie as the surrounding crowd chanted their names. He shimmied back to the balcony and hauled himself up. Michael was desperate to get away from the estate and all it represented. First, he needed to retrieve something as precious to him now as it had been twelve years ago.

It took Michael a few minutes to vault seemingly endless balconies as he made his way to the other side of the mansion. He was cautious not to let despair cloud his mind too much and accidentally leap into the sights of a security camera. Eventually, he found himself in front of the window of his old room. Fortunately, it was ajar, and the chamber beyond was dark. He pulled the window open and crawled through.

Michael's eyes took time to adjust to the gloom, but he dared not turn on the lights and risk attracting attention. He tiptoed over to the main door and found it locked. They had literally forgotten about him and thrown away the key. He saw the furniture covered with white sheets to guard against dust. Michael felt a chill as he suddenly imagined himself to be a ghost wandering through the space of a past life, all traces erased. However, he knew at least one part of him remained, for only he carried the secret. He stepped over to a panel in the wooden wall close to his old bed and gave it a hard thump at the base.

The panel gave way slightly, enough for Michael to insert fingers through a gap that appeared and pull. The wooden square came away to reveal a hidden alcove. Michael reached inside and pulled out his old backpack. He opened it to check the contents were intact, though he was sure they would be. Not long after settling into the Trelane mansion, a young Michael had found the loose panel and the hiding place behind it. It acted as a depository to safeguard the items of emotional value left by his mother. It also helped hide what was left of her from seeing the man Michael had become. By concealing his keepsakes, he also sought to bury the guilt they evoked, a feeling that initially gnawed until his self-justification - no, self-deception - eased his conscience.

Michael felt inside the backpack and found the matted fur of his cuddly lion and the crinkled surfaces of the landscape posters. He sighed in relief but struggled to hold back a sudden urge to weep. He felt sorry for himself, but it was more than that. Years' worth of repressed emotions stirred from their slumber and cried out to be freed. But now was not the time.

Michael zipped up the backpack, slung it over his shoulder and replaced the panel as if nothing was amiss. He returned to the window, stopped, and checked the mantlepiece. The photograph of Sarah was gone. Like everything else of his, it had been removed from the room. Michael could have searched the mansion, but he knew it to be a fool's mission. The photo could have been in Charlie's study, Huxley's room, or used for target practice by Sinderella. No, Michael would have to swallow the pain of losing at least one precious item and take consolation in recovering the rest. Yet, there was some hope. The contents of his backpack were reminders of a past that could never be returned to. However, Sarah was a part of his present and perhaps now that Michael had at last found the courage to walk away, she could be part of his future.

12

BROKEN

Michael waited at the entrance to a side alley for hours. It was mid-morning, and after making a swift departure from the Trelane estate, he used the remaining sovereigns stolen from the pimp to transport himself to the only place he could think to go. Michael desperately wanted to see Sarah, hold her, talk to her, and tell her all the things that should never have been left unsaid.

At their last encounter, she had spoken of a crummy apartment on the outer edges of the Gauntlet. However, the only address Michael remembered from sending a letter to her belonged to the community organisers she worked for. Those offices were across the street from where he had waited since just before dawn.

Despite the miracle drugs coursing through Michael's veins, fatigue had finally started setting in. The lack of food was taking a toll. The urge to rest his eyes for a few minutes was increasingly hard to resist. He shook the feeling away and rubbed his face aggressively. He couldn't risk letting Sarah slip by again. A couple of hours earlier, she had entered the office with a steaming disposable coffee cup in one hand and a briefcase in the other.

Seemingly eager to start the day, Sarah had quickly ascended the stairs of the old brownstone building before Michael had a chance to dash across the road. He couldn't simply walk in and ask to see her after vanishing for three months. He also doubted that his unkempt beard, soiled clothing, and generally frazzled appearance would have helped persuade Sarah's colleagues to leave her alone with him.

Finally, just when walking in regardless looked increasingly appealing, Sarah re-emerged from the building. Michael hadn't noticed before, but she primarily wore black. Her outfit consisted of a tasteful short skirt, heels, jacket and overcoat, with a white blouse the only differing colour. The setup complemented her raven hair, loose strands of which blew in the breeze, which she brushed back into place with gloved hands. Even as Dominion City entered spring, its position on the northern coast of the Imperium meant it was still prone to cold snaps. Still, Michael had rarely seen Sarah wearing such sombre attire. She usually embraced colour, even when the prestigious law firm of her early career prized sober professionalism.

Michael followed Sarah from a distance as she walked down the street. Her hands were planted in the pockets of her overcoat, meaning she had left her briefcase at the office and wherever she was heading was likely only a temporary destination. Michael's pursuit continued for almost ten minutes as he waited for the right opportunity to engage.

He was aware they were going deeper into the Gauntlet, albeit into an area nowhere near as bad as the neighbourhood Michael had grown up in and found himself unceremoniously dumped the previous night. The streets they now navigated were simply deprived rather than rough, populated by residents still trying to maintain a quiet dignity in the face of adversity.

Eventually, Sarah stopped at a small convenience store sandwiched between apartment blocks and entered. Michael took cover behind a nearby lamppost and tried to examine the shop from a distance as best he could. It seemed to cater to various requirements, with brooms, mops and other domestic tools stacked outside and canned goods and fresh produce visible in the windows.

The glass itself was miraculously free of wire mesh, indicating a degree of trust by the owner that no one would throw something through the window and help themselves to what was inside. To say the area was gentrifying would have stretched the concept to breaking point. Still, Michael was quietly impressed to see clear signs of normality and decency. Perhaps Sarah's efforts to improve local people's lives were indeed paying off.

She emerged a moment later carrying a small bouquet of flowers. Curious, Michael resumed his stealthy pursuit. After another few minutes, Sarah crossed the street and entered what looked to be a park enclosed by a high surrounding wall. Fortunately, other entrances were built into the barrier, their iron gates wide open. Michael chose one a fair distance away from Sarah's point of entry so as not to arouse suspicion, not that she exhibited any signs of it. If anything, she seemed lost in her thoughts.

As he entered, Michael spotted a plaque confirming that the place had long been a community park and garden, previously left to ruin but since restored thanks to donations from several Golden Gateway companies keen to bolster their public images. Michael suspected that Sarah's charm and social connections had played no small role in encouraging the donations.

The park grounds vindicated the amount spent on salvaging them. It was an oasis of greenery amid the moody urban sprawl, with well-tended grass and clean cobblestone paths. Now that spring was coming into bloom, flowerbeds erupted into kaleidoscopes of colour. Several dozen trees were clustered at the centre to form a micro forest. Some of them had bare branches yet to sprout leaves, whereas others were a variety of evergreens that had not shed during the winter. Birdsong provided a soothing soundtrack, covering up the distant noise of traffic already dampened by the high park walls.

It was late morning on a workday, so Michael spotted only a few homeless or people sitting on benches taking an early lunch break. A hunched-over retired gentleman wearing a long black trench coat, its collar turned up to guard his face against the chill breeze, tossed breadcrumbs from a paper bag at eager pigeons gathered at his feet.

Michael cautiously followed Sarah into the cluster of trees. He wondered as to the purpose of her visit. Was she meeting someone? Otherwise, why come to such a unique place? If that was the case, then he needed to act quickly. At least the cover of the trees would provide some privacy for a reunion. Michael had no idea what he would say. It was just important that he see Sarah, that she would know he was okay and had not simply vanished without a trace. To look into her hazel eyes again was all that mattered.

Michael watched his step, careful to make the minimum sound possible. The last thing he wanted was to snap a twig and cause Sarah to think an unkempt hobo was stalking her. But then, how exactly would he engage? Walking up, tapping her on the shoulder and saying hello seemed inadequate. Michael realised he was overthinking things like at Sam's Coffee Emporium three months prior. He decided to just see what happened and roll with it.

Michael concealed himself behind a large trunk and peered around it. He found Sarah standing in front of a young tree, perhaps only a meter or so in height, a few leaves clinging to its thin branches. She was a dozen feet away, easy enough to reach in a few broad steps, but something compelled Michael to wait, as if she were in a private moment that he dare not disturb.

'I'm sorry it's taken me this long to see you,' she said, maintaining her gaze on the tree.

Michael glanced around, sure that the person Sarah had come to meet had suddenly shown up, but it remained just the two of them. He carried on listening.

'If I'm honest, I put it off because I hoped I'd forget and move on with my life. But I was just fooling myself. I couldn't ever move on until I said what I needed to say. Getting the money to fix this place up may be a good memorial, but it's not a goodbye.'

Michael felt his stomach lurch, even more so than when witnessing Charlie's public praise for Huxley. His growing fear was confirmed when Sarah knelt down and gently rested the bouquet of flowers at the base of a small upright marble plaque erected in front of the young tree.

Some cultures around the world buried their dead, but custom in the Imperium was cremation and the spreading of ashes at the roots of trees so that, in a sense, part of the deceased would live on and grow, nourished by the comforting light of Holy Sol. Once again, it seemed that Mears's wonder treatments had fixed more than just Michael's muscles and bones, as his eyes could sharply focus on the plaque's engraving without even trying.

Here Grows Michael Ryan
In Loving Memory
A Good And Decent Man
Even If He Didn't Realise It

Everything crystallised in Michael's head. He had not gone unmentioned in Charlie's victory speech because he was considered missing and easily dismissed. It was because the world believed him dead, including the woman who knelt only feet away, struggling to contain tears that started to flow and would not stop.

'Damn it, why didn't you come with me?' she yelled at the plaque as if it was expected to offer an explanation. 'I can't promise it would have worked, but at least you'd be alive. All I wanted was for you to be the man I knew you could be, whether we were together or not. Now it's too late.'

As Sarah wiped tears from her cheeks, Michael could no longer contain his anguish. He was about to step out from behind the trunk when he noticed a figure approach her from the side, coming from the opposite direction to Michael's hiding spot. He suppressed a gasp as he saw Huxley stand next to her, holding his own bouquet of flowers. Sarah glanced up, unsurprised. She had been expecting him.

'Hello Sarah,' Huxley said gently. 'I didn't mean to intrude.'

'It's okay,' she replied with a sniff, composing herself as she stood up. 'It's the first time I've come here, and I didn't think I'd find it so hard.'

'I know how you feel,' responded Huxley in sympathy. He leaned down and placed his own flowers next to Sarah's. 'I miss him every day.'

'The last time I saw Michael, the two of you had just been in a brutal fight,' noted Sarah with a sceptical tone.

'Things got a little out of hand, that's all,' shrugged Huxley. 'You know what it's like at the House, how egos can get in the way of things. It doesn't mean I didn't love and respect Michael.'

Michael again felt the anger rise in him, the kind he knew would become uncontrollable. The desire to stride out, take Huxley by surprise and smash his head against the gravestone of the man he thought he had killed but professed to love was overwhelming. Huxley's feigning of loss was galling, but Michael knew it came from the same playbook that had blinded Charlie and numerous others to the monster that lurked beneath the charming facade.

'Look, thank you for coming today,' said Sarah. 'I wanted to tell you in person how much I appreciated your help in having Michael's ashes delivered here.'

Ashes? That meant there must have been a body identifiable as Michael's in the ruins of the warehouse. He quickly surmised that it was well within Loman and the Covenant's ability to manufacture convincing evidence or alter the coroner's report.

'There's no need to thank me for doing the right thing,' said Huxley with faux humility. 'I know how you feel about your dad and the House, Sarah, but please believe I'm doing my best to honour Michael's memory by turning it into something that I hope he and, in time, you can be proud of.' He placed a hand on Sarah's shoulder. 'Whatever your feelings, I promise I'll always be there for you, no matter what.'

Huxley drew Sarah into a warm embrace and Michael screamed inside. He was compelled to act and balled up his shaking fists. Just as he was about to launch himself with violent abandon, he suddenly felt a hand come from behind and rest on his shoulder. Whoever it was must have floated above the ground, as Michael had sensed no approach. An instant later, a familiar voice whispered in his ear.

'If you act now, he will surely kill her to protect his lie,' said Loman.

The urge to strike remained undimmed, but Loman squeezed Michael's shoulder and subtly, but noticeably, pressed down to make it harder to rise. It simultaneously felt like a gesture of support and restraint.

'Wraiths are forged in the fire of adversity,' Loman continued, his whisper so soft as to be almost imperceptible. 'You awoke with new eyes to see the pain inflicted on the weak and the innocent. Those you thought of as family have forgotten you like a discarded tool, as is the way with their kind. Now the world considers you dead if you decide to remain so. I offered you a choice, Michael Ryan. It is now yours to make.' He withdrew his hand.

Every fibre of Michael's being screamed at him to do something. He felt like he was standing in front of an open barrel of gunpowder holding a naked flame. All he needed to do was toss it in and witness the unfolding destruction. His dark side willed him to do it, consequences be damned. Michael squeezed his eyes shut so tightly as to almost hurt. It may have only been seconds, but it felt like an age as impulse battled reason. Gradually the fire inside diminished. It was not extinguished, but it was enough for Michael to reassert control. He opened his eyes and peered around the tree trunk to see Sarah and Huxley part from their embrace.

'Thank you, Dominic, it means a lot,' she said absently, her thoughts elsewhere. 'Can I ask you something, please?'

'Of course, anything at all,' he replied positively.

'How exactly did Michael die?'

Huxley looked taken aback by the question but quickly recovered.

'I won't lie, Sarah, as painful as it'll be to hear. I'll tell you the same thing I told your father. Michael and I were trying to negotiate a peace deal with the Littmans after they attacked us without reason. Some of Charlie's advisors wanted to go to war, but Michael and I were determined to try and avoid it, even if it risked our own safety. As it was, our meeting at the warehouse turned out to be an ambush. Littman's men attacked, and a firefight broke out. Michael was hit. I tried to get to him, but there were too many bullets. Then someone must have started a fire because flames came out of nowhere. I did all I could, but I just couldn't save him.'

Huxley closed his eyes and shook his head despairingly, pretending to relive a painful memory. Michael found the display sickening and impressive in equal measure, almost in awe at Huxley's ability to spin a conveniently heroic fantasy out of the dark, treacherous reality. No wonder Charlie had moved on, having been convinced his protégé had died a noble death in service to him. Loman was right. If Michael's survival was revealed, Huxley's entire house of cards would collapse. He would hunt Michael until the job was finished, and no doubt Sarah would also feature high on his hit list if she discovered the truth. Huxley opened his eyes and sighed.

'If it's any comfort, I'm positive Michael lost consciousness from his wounds before the fire got to him. I lost my brother that night, Sarah. When I got your message asking for his ashes to be laid to rest here, it was the least I could do to honour his memory.'

Sarah stared at Huxley a moment. Michael couldn't see her expression from behind, but he knew her legal mind was weighing up what she had just heard. However, her silence betrayed nothing.

'Thank you again, Dominic,' she said eventually. 'I just wanted to hear it for myself.' She looked down one last time at Michael's grave. 'Goodbye,' she whispered.

Sarah turned and started walking back in the direction of the main park entrance.

'Are you coming?' she asked Huxley.

'I just need a moment alone,' he replied.

She nodded in sympathy and carried on. Huxley crouched next to Michael's grave. He spoke quietly enough not to risk Sarah catching his words, but Michael remained within earshot.

'I've won, Mikey. Stone cold victory. The House will be mine, this city will be mine, and sooner or later, Sarah will be mine. Once she gets a taste of me, you won't even be a memory.' Huxley checked to make sure Sarah hadn't turned and quietly spat on Michael's grave. 'Rest in peace,' he concluded with a smirk.

Michael watched numbly as Huxley stood, caught up with Sarah and put an arm around her shoulders. He suddenly found himself silently weeping, able to suppress the sound but not the action or the desperate feeling of hopelessness that fuelled it. He again felt Loman lay a hand on his shoulder, but this time he pulled gently, encouraging Michael to stand.

'Your choice is made. For the better, I would say, but the work has only just begun. Come.'

Michael looked on as Sarah walked away in Huxley's arms. He willed her to turn around, but she did not. It looked like she had made her choice too. Michael may have been breathing, the ashes of a stranger absorbing into his grave tree instead, but for all intents and purposes, he was dead. It was time to embrace it and let a new Michael Ryan rise. He stood wearily and turned to face Loman, who was dressed as before, this time accompanied by a long black trench coat with the collar turned up. There were no pigeons surrounding him this time, Michael realised.

Doubtless, Loman had somehow infiltrated the Trelane victory party and observed Michael's actions in the Gauntlet before that. If so, he had gone entirely unnoticed, living up to his Shadow-Wraith moniker. It was all part of some test, Michael supposed, but evidently, one he had passed, for now at least. He was too tired and emotionally drained to take offence at being manipulated. However, Michael had to admit the events of the previous evening and that morning had achieved their purpose. They had successfully burnt all bridges behind him. All that now lay ahead was the unknown road.

Loman stared dispassionately in expectation. Michael wiped his eyes.

'Let's go,' he said firmly.

Sarah suppressed a squirm as Huxley wrapped an arm around her shoulders. She didn't want to seem rude. He was trying to be a comfort, though just as when Huxley embraced her by Michael's grave, he had been a bit too familiar for her liking. Huxley was like a brother as they grew up under the same roof. However, he already had a sister, whom Sarah knew despised her, and she had found a lover in Michael. All that was left for Huxley was friendship.

Sarah wasn't stupid, though, and knew he harboured feelings for her, ones she had never returned and never would. Despite his warm words, Sarah neither needed nor wanted his affections. She had invited Huxley to the gravesite not out of gratitude but to get a straight answer about what happened to Michael in the warehouse. He had offered an explanation, but how much truth it held was another matter. Huxley was always difficult to read, only prepared to show the world what he wanted it to see. Either way, she hoped he would leave her alone going forward. Her desire to disassociate herself from her past life remained undimmed. Nothing could bring Michael back now, but Sarah hoped that she could at least honour his memory through her community work, such as the rejuvenated park. Well, if not the memory of who he was, then at least in honour of who he could have been had he chosen a different path.

She felt better for having finally visited, but throughout her pilgrimage to Michael's grave, Sarah experienced the strange feeling that somehow he was there in spirit, watching over her. Not being superstitious, she dismissed such thoughts as simply nerves the closer she got to the grave and the emotions she knew it would stir. Nevertheless, when she said her final goodbye, it just hadn't felt right, almost like it was uttered prematurely, which was ridiculous. Michael was gone and that was the end of it. He would never be forgotten, by Sarah at least. Life would go on, and he would forever remain the stray and vulnerable boy of her memories, even as she grew old. Still, she just wanted to be sure.

Sarah turned for one last look back at the grave.

There was no one there, just as she knew it would be.

13

REBUILT

Michael could barely keep his eyes open, staring out the front passenger window as Loman drove a black SUV in silence. After navigating through many winding and increasingly narrow streets at the edge of the Gauntlet, they entered a dark tunnel with no lighting and a pinprick of light at the other end to indicate an exit. Halfway down, Michael tensed as Loman suddenly swung the car towards the tunnel wall. Instead of hitting brickwork, the SUV continued on, entering a stone tunnel that matched the aesthetics of what Michael remembered from his brief tour of the Citadel.

He glanced at the rear-view mirror to see a wall descend and seal off the secret entrance. Loman had spoken of a spiderweb of passageways reaching into virtually every corner of the city. It was just about tall and wide enough to fit a vehicle, though Michael guessed that horses were the most likely form of transport when the network was originally built.

Loman drove straight for a time. Michael sensed a gentle downward slope taking them well beneath Dominion City, undoubtedly deep enough to go under the Silver River, the main water artery that cut through the city. His loose sense of direction told him they were heading towards the centre of the city, which made sense, as a network needed a hub. The tunnel eventually evened out, then widened after a few more minutes.

They suddenly emerged into a large chamber. Perhaps it had once been a stable, but now the only horsepower on display belonged to the vast collection of sports cars, SUVs and motorcycles parked up in neat rows. They were a mix of the newest models and classic collectables. However, Michael also spotted some old and worn out vehicles more suited to the junkyard. It was a motorised menagerie that suited all needs, whether arriving at a luxury party or blending into traffic on the clogged Dominion City roads while tailing someone. Loman pulled into a gap in one of the rows and turned off the engine. While certainly better illuminated than the tunnel they had transited through, the garage was moodily lit with strategically placed spotlights. Loman turned to Michael, half his face concealed in darkness.

'I'm guessing Vitamin D supplements are mandatory in this place,' quipped Michael.

He surprised himself, as he wasn't feeling particularly jovial after the emotional battering he had taken over the preceding hours.

'My current prescription is rest,' said Loman flatly. 'You'll need it.'

'When do we start?' pressed Michael.

'We already have.'

After exiting the garage and following Loman along several seemingly identical corridors, Michael was introduced to what would be his room. It was as modest and windowless as everywhere else. However, some small tapestries with attractive patterns and colours adorned the walls and were pleasing enough to the eye, while a large wooden wardrobe contained clean clothing. A writing desk with a simple lamp and chair was placed against one of the walls and at the rear of the room was a bed, which Michael was relieved to see wasn't made of stone. A large ceramic bowl rested upon a nightstand along with a jug of water.

'Is that my bath or my toilet?' asked Michael dryly as he dropped his backpack on the bed.

'Bathrooms are down the hall,' replied Loman as he stood in the doorway. 'This won't be locked, as it is your home now. But I would advise against going exploring unless supervised, for now at least. You have the rest of the day to get some sleep.'

'Fine,' said Michael with a nod. 'Now, if I can just get the room service menu and wi-fi code.'

Loman raised an eyebrow and closed the door without a word.

Michael sat on the bed and was unpleasantly surprised to find the thin mattress had no springs beneath it, just the flat wood of the bed frame. However, he was so tired that he was beyond caring. Michael gently slid his backpack under the bed, lay upon the bedsheets without bothering to cover himself, and closed his eyes.

After what felt like seconds, he opened them with a start as he heard gentle knocking against the thick wooden door of the room.

'Give me a break, I'm only just getting to sleep!' Michael groaned.

'Actually, you've been snoring for over eight hours,' said a male voice beyond the door. This one was new, belonging to neither Loman nor Mears. Michael sat up, curious.

'Come in.'

The door opened with a creak to reveal a young man similar in age to Michael. He was tall and reedy, slightly pale, with a thick mop of dark blonde hair. He was dressed in long shorts that covered his knees, sandals, and a top that had *I graduated from DIT and all I got was this awesome t-shirt* printed on the front. He wore a pair of rectangular wire-rimmed spectacles through which he observed Michael as keenly as Michael studied him. The new arrival also carried a tray upon which rested a bowl of stew, with side portions of cheese, bread and a can of soda.

The pair stared at each other for a moment until Michael cleared his throat.

'Can I help you?'

The young man suddenly broke into a broad grin, slightly embarrassed.

'Ah, of course! Sorry, I'm the one doing the helping, or more accurately the serving,' he said. The visitor shuffled over to the writing desk and set down the tray. 'Dinner, that is.'

'Wait,' said Michael as he rose from the bed. 'Did you say I've been asleep all day?'

'That's right,' confirmed the young man with an eager nod. 'You've been so out of it, I doubt my tranquilliser darts could have done much better.'

'Is that so,' responded Michael dryly as he instinctively rubbed his neck.

The visitor stuck out a friendly hand.

'I'm Felix Harrison, chief technician for the Covenant, as well as IT department, intelligence analyst, general dogsbody, and gifted amateur chef if I do say so myself.'

He nodded proudly at the unappealing brown-coloured stew intended for Michael's dinner. Michael suddenly recalled hearing Mears use the name just after he had emerged from his coma. So far, that made three people, with no indication of anyone else. Was this all the Covenant was?

'Please, call me Felix. Or Fix, if you prefer. You know, just in case that extra syllable is a bother.'

'Felix will be fine. I'm Michael Ryan,' said Michael as he took the young man's hand and shook it firmly. Felix grimaced slightly. 'You okay?' asked Michael as he let go.

'Yes, wonderful,' lied Felix as he shook his hand a little. 'It's just that you're stronger than you remember on account of the compounds we administered during your treatment. Of course, that's nothing compared to what you'll be capable of in your Wraithsuit.'

'Wait, when do I get a suit?' pressed Michael keenly.

'That's out of my hands. I just design it,' replied Felix. 'Along with the rest of the under-appreciated toys we use around here.'

Michael pointed at the slogan on Felix's shirt.

'DIT. The Dominion Institute of Technology, right?' he queried.

'Yes, my old stomping ground, at least until they kicked me out a few years ago,'

'So you never actually graduated?'

'I like to think I graduated in spirit if not on paper,' said Felix slightly defensively before pursing his lips. 'But technically, no, I didn't. I can't really blame them, in fairness. I did accidentally destroy a chunk of the laboratory wing when ambition got the better of my caution.'

'Not to be rude, but how exactly do you accidentally destroy half a building?' probed Michael.

'Easier than you'd think based on some of my experiments,' explained Felix with a shrug. 'But it was that kind of thinking that caused me to end up here. The Covenant was rebuilding and they needed new blood to reinvigorate-'

'What do you mean rebuilding?' interrupted Michael. 'I thought the Covenant was a century old?'

Felix stared for a moment before nervously grinning.

'Yes, that's right. But everything needs a refresh once in a while. Anyway, you'd better eat up. Loman will be coming to collect you in an hour. He expects you to be ready to start training.'

'Seriously?' scoffed Michael. 'It must be, what, eight in the evening?'

'Nine o'clock, actually,' corrected Felix. 'But as you may have noticed from my skin tone, we're nocturnal animals here. Monsters come out at night to play. Well, so do Wraiths.'

Michael stood in the vast chamber he had been told was called the Gymnasium, though it looked like none he'd ever seen. There may have been a few cardio-vascular machines and weights benches in the corner, but they felt like an afterthought compared to the room's highlight. Dominating the Gymnasium was a comprehensive, multi-tiered obstacle course, which surrounded the large circle of rubber matting Michael stood upon. The obstacles were arranged on four sides, forming a square.

After making his way through Felix's surprisingly tasty stew, Michael had showered and shaved. He had traded his dirty clothing for a fresh pair of lycra shorts, a vest top and training shoes. New clothing, smooth skin and a full stomach worked wonders. He felt ready and enthused about taking on whatever challenge Loman had in store. Still dressed in black as he ever was, the man himself stood a few feet in front of Michael, hands clasped behind his back.

'You have skills, Michael, that is clear, whether in movement or combat,' began Loman. 'However, they are raw and unshaped. Even the most powerful weapon has no utility if it is not used properly and directed at the right target.'

'I've done okay for myself,' challenged Michael.

'Okay is not good enough at this level,' retorted Loman. 'You succumb to your emotions too easily, like when Huxley defeated you in the burning arena.'

'You saw that?'

'Yes, and I wish I hadn't. It was frankly an embarrassment. Suppose you had kept calm and considered your situation with cold reason, staying above the fray and base instinct. In that case, the outcome might have been different. But your rage took over, bringing you down to Huxley's level, which he was always the master of. As soon as that happened, he played you like a flute.'

Michael bit his tongue. He knew Loman was right, though he was loath to admit it. That said, he wasn't prepared to weather all criticism.

'At least I didn't rip his head off back at my grave. That was a nice trick, by the way. What poor fool got cremated instead of me?'

'Just one of the countless victims of your former fraternity, a homeless drug addict that regrettably no one will miss, but in death provided some noble service that eluded him in life,' answered Loman. 'Manipulated bureaucracy and dental records completed the illusion.'

'That's cold, Loman,' said Michael, shaking his head.

Loman narrowed his eyes and started to slowly walk around Michael.

'Coldness has its place, and so does rage. Understand me, I did not say it had no role, just that it must be honed, controlled, and applied precisely, not emotionally. In fact, we could use a little righteous fury. For too long, the criminal and the corrupt have held sway. The Covenant retreated into the shadows and left the rot to take hold.'

'Was this during the period of rebuilding I've heard about?' probed Michael. Loman's stride slowed slightly, but he betrayed nothing.

'There were times of difficulty not so long ago, but those need not concern you now. We look only to the future and what we can set right. It became clear to me that, my age notwithstanding, operating only from the shadows was failing to hold back the tide. There are increasingly few who even know of the existence of the Wraiths, yourself included until recently. I disrupted where I could, but these days urban legend and myths become so easily entwined with fake news, social media and scepticism. If there is no belief in the existence of the Wraiths, then there is no reckoning with our power and so no fear of the consequences. Just as coldness and rage have their uses, the shadows will always have theirs. But times such as these call for something stronger, more elemental. Sometimes to clear away the detritus, a storm is required.'

Loman stopped in front of Michael and leaned in slightly. His eyes were capable of boring into any soul they deemed fit to examine.

'Perhaps with you, Michael Ryan, we shall unleash one.'

In the days that followed, Michael experienced levels of exhaustion he had no idea were possible, but sheer stubbornness drove him on. He had undertaken the square-shaped obstacle course more times than he could remember, reducing his completion time incrementally with every circuit. Loman was nearby, a stopwatch in hand. His blunt bellowing of times was quickly followed by 'not good enough', 'faster' and, consistently, 'again'.

The obstacle course itself was simple in design yet complex in execution, a testament to Felix's mechanical skills and fiendish imagination. The first side of the square started with a series of extremely narrow ramps with increasingly harsh angles which needed to be hopped between and scaled. These elevated Michael from ground level to several dozen feet above the gymnasium floor, certainly high enough to hurt and risk a fracture if he fell.

From the top of the final ramp, practically vertical, Michael used the momentum to jump to the first in a row of monkey bars. After making short work of them, he launched himself from the final rung. He landed on a small square platform fixed atop a tall metal pole, which marked the beginning of the second quarter of the square. Michael tackled half a dozen similar platforms at different elevations and then leapt to the first in a trio of climbing ropes.

He grabbed it and swung like an ape from one to the next. He released from the third rope at just the right time to land on an artificial climbing wall at the beginning of the third side of the square. It was the trickiest obstacle up to that point, for if Michael misjudged the placing of his hands and feet as he hit the wall, he would painfully smash against the side and fall to the padded crash mats below.

When he reached the top of the climbing wall, Michael heaved himself onto an unstable platform. It was hinged at its centre and rocked like a seesaw, making it impossible to hold in place without supreme balance. He didn't have time to linger anyway, as aside from soliciting a rebuke from an observing Loman, pausing would have just encouraged Michael to hesitate in the face of the next obstacle.

Three large cylinders rotated clockwise, counter-clockwise and clockwise in turn. Their smooth, polished surfaces did not even provide a rudimentary grip for his training shoes. They had claimed him several times, causing Michael to plummet to the crash mats below. Loman had been typically unsympathetic, pointing out that the real world had no padding, and perhaps removing such protection would focus Michael's mind a little more.

Determination to conquer the cylinders was motivation enough for Michael, and gradually he perfected his technique. The key was not to overthink the movement and execution but to do as he did with parkour and just flow. He leapt to the first cylinder, let it carry him for a heartbeat, and then jumped to the second. He placed one foot on its surface, the downward pressure of all his weight mitigating against the slippery surface for a split second. It was enough to allow Michael to channel sufficient energy into that leg to launch himself off the second cylinder and plant the other foot onto the third and final roller. He maintained just enough balance to be carried forward until it was optimal to leap and land upon the next immediate challenge.

It was a conveyor belt that continuously advanced forward at speed. Wooden beams with padded tips would snap out from nearby boxes at different angles and elevations, attempting to knock Michael off. He had successfully ducked and dived during his first few attempts to avoid a jab to the head or a beam sweeping at his feet, only to receive a winding blow to the stomach or knock to the knee. There was no pattern to the beams, which prevented memorising any sequence. So Michael prepared himself for painful randomness each time he took on what Felix had amusingly christened the 'Disassembly Line'.

Michael's reactions had been helped immensely by the supplements supplied by Doc Mears. The latter had visited several times to confirm that not only had Michael been restored to his former health but that he was now surpassing it. He had the heart of an ox, his bones were healed completely, and his muscle mass and definition would have been the envy of any elite athlete.

'These aren't going to make my balls shrink to the size of raisins, are they, Doc?' Michael had queried, impressed with the results but wary of the consequences.

'Don't worry,' Mears reassured as he handed over a tiny cup of pills to swallow. 'There's nothing dubious about them. These are highly concentrated vitamins, minerals and amino acids, along with natural compounds derived from certain plants found in the Tetcheho jungles. They've all been enhanced in labs using artificial intelligence-driven sequencing. The results turbocharge your metabolism, recovery and healing, muscle mass and bone density, and amplify your natural senses and brain functions. Think of them as evolution in a pill, if you like.'

'And these labs of yours, I'm guessing they're not at the Citadel or in your spare room?'

'The Covenant has privileged access to early research and development projects at various pharmaceutical and technology companies, though you can credit Felix for a lot of the toys you'll be using. However, that early look allows us months, if not years, of advantage. What you've been swallowing is destined for Special Forces soldiers when it's finally signed off.'

That caused Michael to pull a double-take.

'Wait, what? These things are still experimental?'

'Don't worry,' said Mears as he raised a hand for calm. 'I've thoroughly analysed the data and I'm satisfied they're safe, but you know how long the regulators can take these days. That being said, if you start to sprout leaves from anywhere sensitive, do let me know.'

Mears's wry grin indicated the good doctor had been joking. However, Michael still checked himself in the mirror more frequently.

Risk of sprouting foliage or not, Michael couldn't deny the results. Other than the obvious physical benefits, he indeed felt more mentally agile. He found he could easily recall even minor details from a conversation or incident months prior, replaying them in his head as clearly as if he were watching a recording. He was alert to the quietest noises, such as the buzzing of a fly or the light tapping of a mouse's feet against stone flooring. When it came to reaction times, Michael was appreciably sharper. It sometimes felt like fast-moving events were moving in slow motion. Such heightened awareness gave him an edge when tackling the Disassembly Line.

As the floor of the conveyer belt advanced, Michael took the initiative and ran forwards rather than passively wait for the beams to strike. The first snapped out in front of him at chest level. Michael leaned back hard and let the belt carry him under the beam with an inch to spare. He instinctively knew another one would be incoming, and a second later, it swept low to take out his feet. Michael was ready and executed a spotless backflip, immediately followed by a forward diving roll that launched him over a third beam that struck out at waist height.

Before he knew it, Michael had reached the end of the conveyer belt and was out of danger, having rapidly sped through the potential hazards. He supposed there was a lesson he was meant to learn. Being overly cautious and hesitant allowed time for dangers to gather, perhaps too many to fend off, while taking the initiative by racing forwards reduced the opportunities to be knocked off. Alternatively, Loman and Felix had taken a perverse joy in throwing everything at Michael to see how he would handle himself, which was just as plausible.

At the end of the Disassembly Line, Michael reached the fourth and final side of the obstacle course. After the slippery rollers and conveyer belt of punishment, the challenge of navigating two dozen poles of increasingly shrinking diameter seemed almost quaint. There were no flat square platforms atop them as before, simply the smooth tops of the poles themselves. The first had the diameter of a modest tree, while the last would have barely accommodated a golf ball. With no place to linger once the conveyer ended, Michael had no choice but to leap to the first pole and gain his balance. As with all other elements of the course, he couldn't afford to pause for long. He was up against the clock, and a dissatisfied Loman would simply make him do it all again unless he delivered an improved time.

As with the rollers, Michael didn't pause to overthink. He leapt from the top of one pole to another, ignoring the discomfort in his soles as less surface area increased the pressure on his feet. At the final pole, he was virtually on tiptoes and felt like a ballet dancer. Ahead was a smooth metal slope that would carry him down to the Gymnasium floor and the finish line.

Michael jumped, landed on his rear and slid down with increasing speed. All the while, he saw Loman keeping a keen eye on his stopwatch. A few seconds later, Michael hit the ground, rolled and stood upright in front of his timekeeper. He waited expectantly, trying to pace his breathing to not betray how exerted he was.

Loman glanced up from the stopwatch, his expression impassive.

'Acceptable,' he said.

Michael couldn't help but grin in satisfaction that he had beaten his previous best time. He had quickly realised that a monosyllabic response was the best he would get from Loman by way of validation.

'There is always room for improvement in everything we do,' continued Loman. 'But I think we can move on to the next challenge.'

Michael betrayed nothing and simply nodded but was pleased to put the obstacle course behind him. Loman clapped his hands twice in quick succession, and the Gymnasium was plunged into darkness as the lighting shut off.

'Again.'

Michael grimaced as Felix tightly fastened the last strap of the training suit. It was a bulky, form-hugging outfit of black leather and thick pads located at various points around his body. Felix had explained that the suit would do a generally good job of mimicking the weight and feel of Michael's future Wraithsuit, so he may as well get used to it. As for the strategically placed pads, they contained sensors that would detect if a hit landed during the training simulation that was about to begin.

Loman stood close by on the edge of the circular sparring area at the centre of the Gymnasium, quietly observing. Felix handed Michael a fighting staff. It was similar in length and weight to the one he had used to duel with Huxley back at Charlie's birthday celebration. Instead of smooth wood, it was something altogether more high tech. It was black and looked metallic but felt light and robust.

'I'm told you handle one of these reasonably well,' said Felix.

'It's not a stranger,' replied Michael as he twirled it.

'It might not be a stranger, but it still brings a couple of surprises to the party,' continued Felix as he pointed to one of two subtle oval-shaped buttons at the centre of the pole. 'Go on, try it.'

Michael obliged, and the pole extended a foot in each direction, providing extra reach if needed. He admired it with approval.

'Hold down the same button and it'll retract to half the original size, making it nicely portable for stowing on your back. Now try the second button.'

Michael did so, and the pole retracted in length before splitting in two. Surprised, he grabbed the second of what had become a pair of billy clubs before it hit the rubber matting. Felix grinned in satisfaction.

'Two for the price of one. When you're done, simply attach both ends together and twist, and it'll become a staff again.'

Michael nodded, impressed. He did as Felix instructed, and the two batons became one again. Felix knelt next to a nearby hard-plastic case, opened it, and produced a pair of wrap-around shades. He gently slid them onto Michael's face, and the room went a little darker.

'What's this?' asked Michael.

'The latest in augmented reality. Are they comfortable?'

Michael nodded, and Felix pressed a small button on the frame. The Gymnasium, Felix and Loman instantly disappeared and were replaced by a flat urban rooftop belonging to some kind of high-rise building. In the background, the skyline of central Dominion City was so clear and vivid that Michael felt as if he were standing there for real. He couldn't help but grin.

'Wow, Felix, this is amazing. How do you do it? Felix?'

When no response came, Michael turned to look for the vanished technician and was startled to see a masked ninja dressed all in red running towards him, brandishing a fighting staff. Michael instinctively raised his own to block, but instead of the virtual ninja's staff passing through like the illusion it was, Michael felt the force of the impact.

'What the-' he began, momentarily confused. That confusion rapidly dissipated when the ninja pressed the advantage of surprise, changed position, and jabbed Michael's midriff with the staff. Michael felt every bit of the sharp blow, gasped and backed away.

'What is this?' he called out.

'I told you, the sensors on your suit detect the virtual hits,' replied Felix's disembodied voice.

'You didn't tell me they'd feedback those hits, too!'

'Consider it elevated combat training,' said Loman as he spoke for the first time, his voice equally difficult to locate. 'You already have reasonable combat skills. Here you can perfect your fighting style in any environment and against any opponent you wish.'

'Fine,' said Michael as he and the virtual ninja slowly circled each other. 'Make this guy look like Huxley.'

'This is training, not therapy,' replied Loman. It was clear the answer was no, which irked Michael.

'Then at least give me a proper challenge, a realistic one,' he demanded. 'Criminals cluster together for strength in numbers. They don't fight one on one.'

Loman thought for a moment.

'I dare say some of the more skilled opponents you will face would disagree, but I take your point regarding standard street thugs. Very well.'

After a moment, the red ninja vanished in a whirlwind of pixels, which separated and reconstituted into five huge rough-looking thugs in torn clothing. They sported numerous gangland tattoos, and each carried a manual weapon, such as a club or a crowbar. The five eyed Michael with hatred and started to advance.

'I believe this presents the realistic challenge you requested,' said Loman.

Michael was sure he detected a trace of amusement in the older man's tone but had no time to dwell on it as the five thugs charged toward him, their weapons held high, ready to strike. Michael twirled his battle staff and braced for the onslaught. He felt no fear, only anticipation. For the first time since his life had shattered into pieces, he was beginning to feel whole again.

The chill wind stung Michael's skin, but he didn't mind. He was just glad to be outside, reminded that a world existed beyond the confines of the Gymnasium and the seemingly endless labyrinth of the Citadel. During downtime from training, Michael had used the opportunity to explore, to get a better feel for his new home.

Loman had imposed no restrictions, only that he steer clear of the Catacombs, the entrances to which were clearly marked by removable red barriers. The mysterious underworld beneath the Citadel was not forbidden, but structural issues meant it was regarded as too risky to casually explore without proper equipment. Michael had made a mental note to return when time allowed and instead focused on what lay above the Citadel. Over several weeks he discovered secret exits that opened up into all areas of the city, from an unnoticed manhole cover in a dingy back alley, to a rusted gate that led to Dominion City's expansive sewer system, to a forgotten door in a dusty storage room of a public library.

Michael's recent discovery led to what had quickly become a favoured spot. A trapdoor opened at the base of an old but sturdy watchtower built in the pre-industrial days of the Imperium. It was a testament to how far the capital had expanded over the centuries that a structure that once protected its borders now found itself in a Royal Park next to the Imperial Mile at the heart of the city.

The tower had been preserved as a heritage site, protected by high iron railings but still tall enough that tourists could easily take selfies in front of an impressive relic of Imperial history. Not that Michael risked being photographed, for the park was closed at night, and the gentle spotlights that illuminated the stonework failed to reach all the way to the top.

The commanding view of the city was worth the climb up the tight spiral staircase and exposure to the elements. Leaning upon the chest-high wall at the top, Michael could take in the park's serenity at night and then cast his eye up to the Imperial Mile beyond it.

Towering statues of past rulers were evenly spaced out either side of the immense boulevard while still ensuring plenty of room for their descendants to be added when their reign ended. Michael was not an avid follower of the Royal Court but had scanned enough news websites to pick up rumours of the Emperor's declining health. The chief suspect was cancer, but whatever the ultimate culprit turned out to be, it looked like it would not be long until his statue was erected alongside his ancestors.

The Emperor's granddaughter and heir, the Crown Princess, was protected from the media spotlight by a zealous Imperial Guard, with only a few official portraits suggesting she was in her late teens. Michael turned his gaze from the vast Imperial Palace grounds at one end of the Mile to the grand Congressional Forum building at the other. No doubt the politicians that dwelled in that seat of government would try and incur favour with the new Empress when the time came, or attempt to run rings around a naïve young woman. Michael suspected it would likely be both.

He looked back towards the Palace and stopped halfway along the Mile, his eyes resting on the glimmering Cathedral of Light. For all the gloom and squalor of many parts of Dominion City, Michael could not deny the sheer beauty of the grandest solar temple at its heart. Shafts of golden light surrounded the central dome of the building and reached into the night sky like a beacon for the lost to find their way. Michael had never been a particularly spiritual person, but nor did he rule anything out, and so would never begrudge those who found comfort in worshipping Sol. He had undoubtedly developed a keener appreciation for what might come after death following his all-too-close encounter with it.

Michael's thoughts drifted as he counted the different airships floating above the Imperial Mile or further out near the Golden Gateway and Isle of Dreams. They came in various shapes and sizes, from small police blimps packed with surveillance equipment for crowd monitoring to giant, vaguely cigar-shaped dirigibles with LED screens fixed to their sides that displayed all manner of advertising.

Michael spotted a fuzzy logo for Silver River Craft Beer and suddenly found himself yearning to sit down with a tall frosty glass. He didn't miss the booze itself, as he was never much of a drinker, but more the normality of the act. Simply sitting at a bar and sipping from a bottle held appeal or, more preferably, lounging at Sam's Coffee Emporium with a latte in hand, watching the fire crackle in the hearth. That world was lost to him now, for Michael couldn't risk anyone from his past knowing he was alive, as it would only put them in danger. It quickly became a lonely way to live, but the continuous training provided suitable distraction. However, even that was starting to wear thin, as was Michael's patience.

He heard someone ascending the stone steps and turned to see Felix emerge from the spiral stairway, holding a thermos mug in each hand.

'Coffee?' asked the engineer.

'Sure,' Michael responded. It wasn't Sam's, but it would do.

Felix handed over a mug and stood alongside Michael, taking in the impressive view.

'I can see why you come up here,' he remarked.

'How did you know where I was?' queried Michael.

'We have cameras and sensors at every entrance and exit to the Citadel,' answered Felix. 'You never know when some curious kids or urban explorers looking for their next social media post might stumble across us, given how big the place is.'

'And what happens if they do?'

'Shutting off the lights and pumping out scary noises on the sound system usually does the trick, or I'll dress up as a city engineer and warn them it's too dangerous before they get far. Honestly, though, it's rarely an issue. The Covenant's been doing this for a century. It knows how to keep things hidden.'

'Except when they want something,' remarked Michael dryly. 'Then they're happy to be seen.'

'Yes, I suppose,' conceded Felix as he quietly sipped from his mug.

Michael and the young scientist had engaged in plenty of small talk since his arrival at the Citadel, but the opportunity for a deeper conversation had eluded them. Michael decided to take advantage and pose a question he also intended to ask Loman when the time was right.

'I get why they approached you, given all the useful ideas floating around up there,' said Michael as he tapped his temple. 'My question is, why did you take them up on their offer?'

'Same reason as you, I guess,' responded Felix after a moment.

'Sorry, but I just don't buy that. I have a lot to atone for. Half a lifetime's worth, in fact. You don't strike me as someone with a dark past.'

'Then you'd be surprised,' Felix said bluntly. It was clear Michael had touched a nerve, so uncharacteristic was the response from the consistently affable technician. Felix immediately winced at his reaction. 'Sorry, didn't mean to be rude. We've all made mistakes and not just blowing up labs. I suppose that's why I'm not inclined to get on my high horse about what you've done in your past life. And it's exactly that, a past life. You're here now and looking to do some good, just as I am. That's what I meant by the same reason.'

'I can respect that,' said Michael.

'You know, I always had big dreams as a child, of leaving my mark on the world,' continued Felix as he stared ahead, reminiscing. 'Astronaut, inventor, intrepid explorer, things like that. I consumed every book on science and technology I could find. Physics, chemistry, biology, mechanical engineering, computer science. You name it, I've studied it. I became a jack of all trades *and* a master of all if you'll pardon the self-confidence. But it was all in service to those dreams. Not to become rich and famous, but to be the good I wanted to see in the world.'

Michael swallowed hard at hearing Felix's motivation unknowingly come close to matching his mother's sentiment. Felix downed the rest of his coffee and turned to look Michael in the eye.

'I'm not the biggest or the strongest, but I have power where it counts. I joined the Covenant because I was fed up with living in a world where too many feel that kindness is a weakness. If I can contribute to making it even a slightly better place, it'll have been worth it. That's my reason.'

Felix let silence punctuate his point. Michael simply nodded in understanding. There was no need to dig any deeper. He realised he hadn't even touched his coffee. He flexed his fingers.

'I seem to have more power than I know what to do with, and what good am I actually doing in the world? I spend the whole damn time fighting things that aren't even there.'

'Wrong,' said Loman from behind the pair.

Michael and Felix spun around in surprise. The former Wraith had, appropriately, seemingly appeared from thin air. Even Michael, with his enhanced senses, had failed to detect the older man's stealthy approach.

'Damn it, Loman, that joke's wearing very thin!' exclaimed Michael.

'You say you fight nothing,' continued Loman, ignoring Michael's annoyance. 'Not so. Every day you fight yourself and win. You take on your weaknesses and claim small victories. With each battle, you refine your fighting style, hone your technique, and sharpen your skills so that when the day comes to pitch yourself against more than Felix's digital monsters, you will be ready.'

'I'm ready now,' insisted Michael.

'You think so?' queried Loman, a trace of scepticism in his tone.

'I *know* so,' replied Michael firmly as he detected that doubtfulness and challenged it.

Loman considered his student a moment, then glanced at Felix, who nervously observed the exchange. Loman looked back to Michael and stepped forwards until the two men were face to face. He leaned in slightly and considered his successor through narrowed eyes.

'Then show me.'

14

RUNNING THE GAUNTLET

Michael perched on the edge of a rooftop high above
the main street of the Gauntlet. A day had passed since
Loman had issued his challenge to the would-be Wraith
and there was no better proving ground than Michael's
old neighbourhood, where darkness and desperation
hung in the air as keenly as the pollution.

Felix was still working on creating the new Wraithsuit,
and so for Michael's first solo patrol, he had been
offered what the technician had dubbed the Scoutsuit
instead. It consisted of a jacket and trousers made of
tough figure-hugging black leather, helping Michael
blend in with the dark urban landscape. Rugged boots
gave him grip, while knee and elbow pads and wrist
guards provided some protection. A hood covered his
head, and black cloth concealed his face beneath the
eyes. Dark camouflage paint was daubed over what skin
remained exposed. He flexed his gloves and ran fingers

over the metal studs above the knuckles. The advanced battle staff was the only concession to the equipment he would continue to use when his complete Wraith kit was ready. It was mounted securely in a sheath on his back.

Michael tapped the earpiece that linked him to Felix and Loman at the Operations Centre back at the Citadel. The place was like a military command bunker crossed with a television studio control room. It had dozens of screens and terminals at the operators' disposal, allowing easy access to virtually every camera in Dominion City plus the internet and secret databases of even the most supposedly secure intelligence agencies. Michael only saw it briefly to give him awareness before suiting up and racing off on a motorcycle down one of the Citadel's secret tunnels that opened up near the Gauntlet.

'Comms check. Am I coming through?' asked Michael.

'Loud and clear,' he heard Felix reply.

'The Gauntlet isn't exactly known for a wealth of security cameras, so I don't think you'll see much of me,' said Michael.

'Oh, we'll see everything, don't worry,' responded Felix. 'There are multiple tiny micro-cameras built into your suit.'

'Of course there are,' sighed Michael, realising it had been a forlorn hope that he would be let out for the first time without any supervision. 'I'm sure Loman is sitting pretty with some popcorn.'

'A cup of tea, actually,' Loman responded.

Even transmitted over a distance into his ear, Michael couldn't help but feel slightly intimidated at hearing Loman's sober tone. He knew it wasn't from fear but a desire to prove that his new mentor's faith in him was justified. Praise from a harsh teacher was always worth more than from a soft one. Perhaps Loman sensed some small sign of moral support was in order, as after a moment, he spoke again.

'Remember, this isn't a driving test. There is no pass or fail. The training wheels are off, but you have good instincts. Use them, both from your previous life and your new one.'

Michael understood the inference. He needed to think like the criminal he used to be. In so doing, he could find a suitable target. He closed his eyes and listened to the sounds of the Gauntlet. They were familiar from his youth and recent return; heavy traffic, music blaring from bars and clubs, and drunken arguments. Michael knew what he was trying to source amid the din, however. It had been the reason for choosing the Gauntlet when he was offered any part of the city for his first patrol. He knew it would not disappoint in meeting its quota of misery.

A piercing scream caused Michael's eyes to snap open. The source was not far, perhaps half a block away. He started running, quickly building speed. When he leapt to the next building, he easily covered the fifteen-foot gap, landed, rolled, recovered, and continued. He effortlessly repeated the same move twice more, a testament to the fitness and agility that weeks spent in the Gymnasium had bestowed. A second scream helped Michael locate the source, and he stopped at the edge of the rooftop that overlooked a dark side alley. He was momentarily stunned by what he saw. Below him, he recognised the pimp he had stolen from previously. The vile creature was also abusing the exact same girl as before. Michael had doubted that in the vastness of the Gauntlet, he would stumble upon the duo again. However, in hope rather than expectation, he still carried a reminder of that event in his pocket.

Michael leapt from the rooftop, grabbed a window ledge and dropped down to one directly beneath. He then jumped to the opposite building and landed as quietly as possible on a fire escape, grasped a drain pipe, and silently slid down it like a stealthy firefighter. His discretion evidently paid off, as the pimp had his back to the entrance of the alley and was none-the-wiser to Michael's approach. This time he paid attention to what the abuser was saying to the terrified young girl as he gripped her arms way too tightly.

'You're makin' me do this, Gina. How many times 'ave I got to tell you, customers always gets what they want, no matter how sick. That's why they come to our place, 'cause we're reliable.'

'Please, I can't do those things. It's too much,' pleaded the girl named Gina as she sobbed. 'I can't handle that kind of pain.'

'Course you can,' countered the pimp with a chuckle. 'You just need warmin' up a bit, that's all, and after I'm done with you for embarrassin' me, that sicko will feel like the perfect gentleman.'

'No, please,' begged Gina as she shook her head.

It was futile. The pimp spun her around and started to twist her right arm painfully behind her back. He had no mercy to offer. Neither did Michael. He tapped the pimp on the shoulder.

'Piss off, I'm workin' 'ere,' retorted the pimp without looking back. Michael tapped again. The pimp released Gina and turned around, annoyed.

'Is you deaf or somethin', I said-' he began before stopping at the sight of Michael in his scout suit dangling the pimp's stolen wallet in front of him.

'I just wanted to say thanks for the loan. Now here's the payback, with interest.'

Michael dropped the wallet and took advantage of the pimp's bemusement to land a hard right hook on his jaw. A trail of blood and several teeth flew out of the pimp's mouth as he went flying into the side of a dumpster. He quickly picked himself up and wiped the blood from his mouth as Gina looked on, frozen. Michael was just over six feet in height himself, but the pimp still had a few inches advantage and decent muscle mass.

'I don't care who you are, freak, I'm goin' to take you apart.'

The pimp launched himself with a roar and took several clumsy swings with his fists. Michael easily dodged them and could have carried on doing so all night, so obvious was the thug's fighting style, or lack of. However, Michael didn't have the patience to play around. After avoiding a final misjudged swing, he ducked and sharply jabbed his attacker in the side of the ribs. This caused the pimp to crumple slightly with pain and allowed Michael to get behind him and kick behind both knees. The giant man's legs buckled, and he hit the ground hard. Michael crouched, grabbed the kneeling pimp's right arm and forced it behind his back, exactly as had been inflicted on Gina. The thug cried out as Michael kept pushing the arm upward at an unnatural angle.

'It's okay,' said Michael through gritted teeth. 'You just need warming up a bit, that's all.'

Michael forced the arm up until he heard bones snap and cartilage tear. The pimp screamed in agony, but Michael kept him in it for a few more seconds before letting go. He grabbed the thug and threw him against the nearby dumpster. The villain's head hit it hard enough to leave a dent in the metal. His screams were silenced as unconsciousness immediately overcame him. Michael stepped over, threw open the dumpster lid, picked up the pimp, and tossed him in. He slammed the lid shut and turned to face a shivering Gina.

'Stay back!' she yelped.

'Careful, Michael,' warned Loman through the earpiece. 'Think about what she's just seen you do and put yourself in her shoes.'

'There's no need to be afraid,' said Michael calmly. He stood still and opened his arms wide to show he was no threat. 'I'm not going to hurt you. No one will ever hurt you again.'

His decision to keep a distance seemed to reassure her a little.

'Who are you?' she asked tentatively.

'I'm just here to help,' he replied. 'Now, that trash in the dumpster said something about customers coming to 'our place'. Did he mean the place you two shared or something bigger?'

Gina looked down at the ground and rubbed her arm nervously.

'Why do you want to know?'

'Because if it's just a place for the two of you, you'll never need to go back. But if it's something bigger, then I'm guessing more girls like you need help. You don't have to say anything. Just nod if I'm right.'

After a moment, the girl sheepishly looked up and gently nodded.

'You're very brave, Gina, thank you. Now, I just need to ask one more thing, and then we'll get out of here. Can you show me where this place is?' probed Michael softly.

After again considering the ground for a moment, Gina raised her head and nodded.

Michael stood in the shadows under a broken street light a hundred yards from the apartment building Gina pointed to. She sheltered behind him, wary of even looking at the place. From her stories of abuse and exploitation, he couldn't blame her for shying away from it. Michael, however, could not help but be transfixed as he stared at the building that had once been his home.

As he looked on, an expensive sports car pulled to a stop outside the front entrance. Out climbed a man Michael recognised to be an older and fatter version of the landlord who had kicked him out onto the streets and stolen his mother's possessions to sell. Instead of the greasy shirt and crumpled trousers he used to wear, the landlord was now decked out in a pricey suit. He had so obviously dyed his greying hair an unnaturally dark black as to look ridiculous.

Usually, such an extravagant vehicle would have been stripped to its shell within five minutes in the Gauntlet. Its owner's confidence in its safety indicated he was recognised as an influential player not to be trifled with.

'Do you know that guy?' Michael asked Gina as they watched the landlord bang on the main door a few times before a slit opened up at eye-level to identify him, and he was admitted.

'That's the boss,' whispered Gina, clearly still frightened. 'He leaves his guys to look after the girls but comes over for a freebie sometimes.'

'Well, it'll cost him tonight,' Michael responded.

It was clear that the landlord had decided there was more money to be made by charging clients by the hour rather than tenants by the month. From what Michael remembered, there were six small apartments on each of the three floors. Supposing each girl warranted an apartment but leaving aside one or two for the landlord's men to occupy, that probably meant a minimum of sixteen women held captive.

'How many guys does the boss have under him?' Michael asked.

'I'm not sure,' Gina replied. 'Maybe six, but sometimes more if there's a card game or they're having a party.'

'Okay, stay here. I won't be long.'

'You're not going in there!' she said in disbelief.

'I'm just going to knock politely and have a little talk with them, that's all,' he reassured her.

Michael set off at a determined pace, reached behind his back and drew his battle staff.

'Would you care to share your plan, Michael?' probed Loman over the earpiece.

'I'm just going to have a chat like I said,' responded Michael as he pressed the second button on his staff, and it separated into two billy clubs, which he twirled in his hands.

'Would that be one of those chats that result in many a broken bone?' queried Felix. 'I can see from your suit sensors that your heart rate and adrenaline levels are elevated.'

'Okay, it'll be a very tough chat, then,' admitted Michael as he stopped at the main door, tapped it several times with a club, and retreated a few feet.

'I know I said it was time for the Wraith to emerge from the shadows, Michael,' began Loman. 'But you are facing an unknown number of opponents. There is a time for force and a time to use stealth to your advantage.'

The slit in the door opened up to reveal a pair of curious eyes.

'Not tonight,' said Michael.

The eyes behind the narrow portal widened as Michael used the space between him and the entrance to accelerate and launch into a flying kick. With all his enhanced strength behind it, his boot impacted the door and ripped it off its hinges, flattening the doorman behind. The momentum carried Michael several metres down the entrance corridor. He rode the door like a surfboard, the unconscious doorman dragged underneath. That was one down, anyway.

There was no commentary from either Felix or Loman. The technician likely had no intelligence to offer, and the former Wraith was no doubt watching to see how his successor would handle himself alone. The training wheels were off, after all. Michael had not burst in completely without thought. His priority was to take down the landlord and his men. With that threat dealt with, he could take time to ensure all the girls were rescued. If any clients were around, they would probably flee, fearful of being caught up in what appeared to be a raid. Any who were foolish enough to put up a fight would quickly regret it.

The brothel was not exactly well-lit, with areas either bathed in gloom or subdued red lighting. Perhaps it was designed to set the mood or make it more difficult for clients to be identifiable. Either way, if seeing things clearly was harder for others, it made Michael's job easier.

A confused pimp appeared from around a corner at the rear of the ground floor. He was able to just about register a look of shock before Michael grabbed his head and smashed it through the cheap plaster wall, deep enough to support him in a standing position despite being unconscious. Michael was aware that he was quickly using up his free hits and the landlord and his remaining gang would surely know something was very wrong.

He quickly made for the staircase to the next floor and dashed up two steps at a time. Halfway up, another pimp appeared, a pistol in hand. Michael threw one of his billy clubs, and it hit the thug square in the forehead. As his eyes rolled back into his head, Michael reached him in time to snatch the pistol, grab the pimp's shoulder and pull forcefully, tossing him down the stairs. Another compatriot appeared from one of the doors that lined the nearby corridor. Keen not to lose his second billy club, Michael instead threw the pistol, which spun through the air until its stock hit the gang member in the face. It would hurt but not incapacitate.

The pimp yelled in pain, but it gave Michael the time he needed to scoop up his first club and charge the recovering villain. He landed several rapid blows with both clubs, the last one sending the battered pimp spinning to the floor of the apartment he had emerged from, out cold. A young girl barely out of her teens screamed from the nearby bed. Michael held a finger to his lips, and she immediately stopped. He briefly caught sight of himself in a small mirror and understood why. His black warrior silhouette against the brothel's red lighting must have made him imposing and intimidating. Good, he would use that.

When no other gang members appeared, Michael gauged that the floor was clear and cautiously moved towards the staircase that led up to the top floor. As his shadow crossed the first few stairs, they erupted into splinters as a hail of bullets tore into the worn wood.

'Come get some!' screamed an unseen member of the gang triumphantly.

Based on the angle, sound and rate of fire, Michael concluded that several handguns had unleashed their rounds rather than a machine gun. The shooters were perched above the stairs, likely two or three of them. If Michael attempted to ascend, he would be greeted by a torrent of bullets.

Though the Scoutsuit offered some protection, his cloth mask was inadequate in the event of a headshot. He heard muffled female screams break out in response to the gunfire. Some became clearer as various apartment doors were flung open and, as predicted, clients scuttled out like rats. Michael needed to bring things to a head before the goons upstairs further fortified.

He turned and spotted a window at the end of the hallway. From his time living in the apartment block, he remembered that the window looked out onto a back alley, with the next building only a short jump away. In his mind's eye, he saw himself run at full speed towards the window, smash through, brace himself against the opposite building's wall for a fraction of a second, and launch upwards at an angle and speed that would propel him through the sister window one floor above and take the pimps by surprise.

Michael tucked his billy clubs into the sheath on his back and raced towards the window. He was committed, and the first few seconds went exactly as visualised. He leapt through the window, shattering it as if it were sugar glass, and sailed through the air. Michael angled his body and legs so that both boots planted themselves firmly on the wall of the opposite building while, at the same time, he aimed himself at the brothel's higher target window. He channelled all his strength into his legs and launched towards it. Michael's feeling of triumph over an improvised but well-executed plan instantly evaporated as he realised he lacked the momentum the carry him all the way.

'Oh crap!' he yelled as he hit the wall hard and just about managed to grab the window ledge.

'I admire the ambition, Michael,' he heard Loman comment. 'However, your new abilities regrettably do not include flight.'

'No, but they do include the ability to tell you to get-' began Michael before he was interrupted as the window opened, one of the pimps leaned out, and pointed a handgun in his face.

'Not so clever now, stranger,' the pimp mocked.

Michael sighed. At least the window was open. He hauled himself up with such speed that the pimp was caught by surprise as the top of Michael's head smashed into his nose. He howled and fell back as Michael's momentum carried him through the opening. He landed on top of the fallen pimp and slammed his fist into the villain's face, breaking the already damaged nose and knocking out its owner.

Michael looked up and saw the landlord and one of his remaining thugs standing above the staircase, clutching their own handguns. He dashed towards the lackey, drawing his billy clubs as he went. The thug managed to fire three shots, but Michael knew that hitting a fast-moving target was difficult, even for an experienced shooter, never mind an apparent amateur who was dealing with poor lighting. Michael ducked, dodged and jumped high to dive into a roll, the three rounds missing him by inches. The Disassembly Line was finally proving its worth.

His roll ended just in front of the pimp, and Michael executed a sweeping kick to the thug's legs, sending him crashing to the floor. The pimp raised his gun to try for another shot. Michael knocked it away with a snap of his left billy club while he used his right one to strike the thug hard on the temple and into unconsciousness. Fast and effective. There was no need to complicate things.

The fat landlord looked on in horror as Michael tore through two of his men in seconds, but his face quickly contorted into a vicious snarl.

'You're dead! Do you know who I am?' he raged as he aimed his pistol.

With a sharp flick of his hand, Michael flung a billy club straight and true. It hit the landlord's gun hand as he pulled the trigger, knocking the bullet's trajectory way off. The landlord yelped and attempted to re-aim but suddenly found the dark intruder towering over him. Michael tore the gun from the fat man's hand, grabbed the weasel by his suit lapels, and lifted him a foot off the floor.

'You look like a cheap thug in an expensive suit, to me,' growled Michael.

He flung the screaming landlord through a nearby apartment door, which crashed open from the force of the weight that hit it. Michael stepped over the threshold as he advanced toward the panicking gangster, who desperately tried to crawl away. His attention was immediately caught by a shivering girl, who clung to a grimy blanket to stay warm.

It was not unusually cold, but Michael quickly realised that her condition was less to do with the temperature and more to do with the needle marks on her arms. That was how the pimps ensured the girls did not escape or put up too much resistance. Where was the need to restrain or imprison when their drug dependency would keep them in place well enough? It looked like Gina had been lucky, assigned to be an attractive street walker rather than a resident of the den of debauchery.

It took Michael a moment to realise that the room he found himself in was a warped and dingy mutation of the sanctuary he had enjoyed with his mother all those years ago. A sickly feeling stirred in his stomach as the scale of the defilement sank in. Instead of warm and comforting lighting, there was only a flickering lamp in the corner. The artwork on the walls had been replaced by patches of dampness and stains created by a multitude of bodily fluids.

He shuddered at the spiritual violation of the one place in his childhood he associated with happy memories. However, that was nothing compared to the physical violation of the poor innocents who had dwelled within its walls. He felt his blood boiling. His watchers must have become aware of it too.

'Michael, I know this is awful stuff,' said Felix, trying to sound calm even as the nerves in his voice were obvious. 'But please don't do anything stupid.'

'What makes you think I would do that?' asked Michael coldly as he approached the landlord, who tried to drag his heavy mass into the small adjoining bathroom.

'Because your heart rate and adrenaline levels indicate you're about to explode,' replied Felix.

'I warn you, Michael,' interjected Loman. 'I know it's tempting, believe me, but should you ever take a life, then your days as a Wraith are finished. We must hold ourselves to a higher standard than those we battle. Otherwise, our covenant with society is broken.'

'I hear you,' said Michael flatly, as if he were half-listening.

'Who are you talkin' to?' whimpered the landlord.

'My conscience,' replied Michael as he advanced. 'It's wondering what to do with you.'

He grabbed the landlord's leg, dragged him back along the dusty floor and hauled him up.

'Please, don't hurt me!' the landlord pleaded.

'You know, I'm just as angry with myself as I am with you, for what I became,' spat Michael. 'This place is as good a metaphor as any. Something pure that became corrupted. The only way back is to burn it down. Scorched earth.'

Upon hearing the threat made against his prized asset, the landlord suddenly abandoned his superficial attempt to look pathetic and snarled once again.

'Don't you dare! You 'ave no idea how long it's taken me to build this empire. I ain't havin' no vigilante tosser take it away from me!'

'And I thought we were getting on so well.'

'You do anythin' to me, and I'll hunt you down and tear you to bits like hounds on a fox,' threatened the landlord.

Michael once again lifted the wide-eyed fat man from the floor and pulled him up close.

'Tell your friends there's a new hunter in town, and it isn't you.'

Michael launched the screaming landlord through a nearby window. The man's cries lasted a few seconds until a loud crash caused them to cease.

'Michael, what have you done!' yelled Loman.

Michael calmly approached the broken window and peered over the edge. Down below, the groaning landlord had landed heavily on his sports car, causing the roof to cave in and shattering all the vehicle's glass.

'He'll live,' remarked Michael acidly.

'You knew the car was down there, right?' asked Felix cautiously.

Michael left the question unanswered and turned to the shivering girl who had silently watched events unfold, either too scared or too absorbed by withdrawal symptoms to make a sound. He slowly approached and gently offered her a hand.

'Don't be afraid. I know a place where you'll all be safe.'

Sarah Ross sat at her office desk and reached for her third cup of coffee of the evening. She focused on the grant application forms before her and brought the cup to her lips. It was empty. She sighed, stood and walked over to the coffee maker in the corner of the communal office. To add insult to injury, the heated pot was also empty. She replaced the filter and waited for the pot to fill with the cheapest coffee her organisation could buy. Given that it was late and she had a morning deadline to submit the forms, beggars couldn't be choosers, and caffeine was caffeine.

Wearily rubbing her neck, Sarah wandered over to the large window that overlooked the street and peered outside. She didn't expect to see anything of interest at such an hour. Still, she would occasionally spot a stray cat or urban fox scavenging for food. It was no small surprise then that Sarah was greeted by the sight of a group of young women slowly advancing towards the building. Some wore scanty clothing, while others were protected by nothing more than blankets.

Shocked, Sarah raced down the stairs and burst out the front door. She quickly reached the group and tentatively approached them.

'In Sol's name! Are you okay?' she asked.

She knew it was a ridiculous question, as they had clearly been mistreated, some more so than others, but Sarah couldn't think of the right words just at that moment.

'Are you Sarah Ross?' asked Gina.

'Yes, that's me,' confirmed Sarah with a nod.

'He told us to come here, that you would be able to help us.'

'Who told you?' probed Sarah gently.

Gina turned around to face a tall building across the street and pointed upwards.

'He did. He saved-'

Gina paused and lowered her hand. Sarah looked up to the roof of the building opposite. There was no one there.

Michael crouched on the edge of a building across the street from his former apartment block. It offered a commanding view of the scene below as firefighters battled the flames that consumed the corrupted palace of vice. Meanwhile, the broken landlord and his gang were loaded onto ambulances, handcuffed and escorted by police. The whole street was awash with red and blue lights from the assorted emergency vehicles that filled the road. Michael couldn't remember the last time he'd seen such an effort in the Gauntlet, but was in no doubt that Felix's call to both the authorities and the media had made a difference. Even if no one cared about the slums, it would still do the politicians no good for an entire neighbourhood to burn down and a sex trafficking ring to walk free while a television news crew covered it all.

Michael had ensured all the girls were found and released before he dragged out the unconscious pimps and tied them up, nicely gift-wrapped for the police. Having made sure the building was empty, he then set it ablaze, as promised. It could not be allowed to stand. Michael was in no doubt that dozens more such places existed in the Gauntlet, but at least there was one less around to destroy young lives. He had guided the girls to Sarah's office, confident that she or someone who knew her would be there to take them in. They would be appropriately cared for, testimony could be gathered against the gang, and hopefully, the young women could begin to rebuild their lives. Some might fall by the wayside, but at least they had hope now and the chance of a brighter future.

Ultimately, that was all that could be asked for. Hope and a chance. It was something Michael now had, but he was also aware that, like the girls, he was at the start of his journey. With the night's events, a small part of his life's ledger had been balanced for the better, but there was still so much to do before he could truly claim to be in equilibrium with the world.

15
THE CALLING

Loman slapped down the morning edition of the Dominion Tribune newspaper in front of Michael, who quietly considered the headline as he sipped a strong coffee. **MYSTERIOUS BLACK GHOST UNCOVERS SEX TRAFFICKING RING, SAVES 17 MISSING GIRLS.**

'Black Ghost?' observed Michael with a raised eyebrow. He shrugged. 'Close enough for now.'

'This is just one paper,' said Loman. 'Others are still coming in, but safe to say you made the front page on all of them.'

'And for those of us who don't kill trees to stay informed, the news sites and social media are on fire with this story,' chimed in Felix.

The three were in the Workshop, yet another of the Citadel's many specialist chambers. This one was most certainly Felix's domain, with various computer terminals, machine tools, 3D printers, workbenches, and even an inspection pit and hydraulic lift for vehicles at his disposal. Loman had interrupted Felix explaining to Michael how long it would take to manufacture his Wraithsuit and what input he needed from its wearer to finalise the design.

Michael considered Loman brooding over the Tribune's headline.

'I didn't realise being sworn to permanent dissatisfaction was part of the Wraith code,' he prodded. 'What's the problem? You said it was time to come out of the shadows, to stir things up. Well, here's proof on paper. What more do you want?'

Loman looked up from the newspaper and gazed at Michael just long enough to be unsettling.

'Nothing,' he said eventually. 'You did good.'

'Well, thanks, I'm flattered,' responded Michael, taken aback by what sounded like praise.

'I said you did good, as in a good deed. Your performance was… adequate.'

'And there it is,' sighed Michael.

'Don't expect things to get any easier,' said Loman sternly. 'Beating up a bunch of common thugs is a low bar to clear, especially given your training and abilities. Hunting such small game, especially when your full battle suit becomes available, will be beneath you.'

'Maybe so, but I know seventeen young women waking up this morning who'll be pleased that I settled for such small game,' Michael retorted.

'Of that, I am sure. Take the win, Michael. I do not begrudge it. Just be aware that not all victories will come so easily or without sacrifice. Now, please excuse me. I have personal matters to attend to.'

Loman nodded and exited without a further word. Michael glanced at Felix.

'Is this what I have to look forward to as a Wraith? My predecessor lecturing me all the time?'

'He has good reasons for caution,' responded Felix. 'You have great power already, and that's just with your battle staff and the Scoutsuit. Throw in your finished

Wraithsuit and some of the other toys I can cook up, and that's a pretty potent force ready to be unleashed. He just wants to make sure you're responsible enough to wield it for the right reasons.'

'In other words, I shouldn't get too cocky,' said Michael.

'Wise words for us all, I think. I mean, my overconfidence did blow up half a building.'

'Point taken.'

Felix cleared his throat, a not-so-subtle signal to change the topic.

'So, we were about to discuss the design for your suit,' he said. 'Let's get to work, shall we?'

Felix rolled his chair over to a sleek computer terminal with three large high-definition screens. He picked up an electronic pen and used a tracking pad to navigate the design software. He tapped a few times to open the relevant file, and a schematic for a generic-looking battle suit appeared. There were no distinguishing features, just a grey-coloured outfit that looked like an armoured jumpsuit.

'Well, we have to go black for a start,' said Michael.

'And there was me thinking pink was the seasonal look for ghostly vigilantes these days,' remarked Felix. 'Any thoughts on your name and symbol yet?'

Michael focused on the slowly rotating virtual suit and all the possibilities open to him. His choices would determine his identity as the Wraith, from look to fighting style. They were not to be taken lightly. He was effectively constructing the other half of his new self, and both sides had to complement each other, not compete. He needed to be true to his nature and the forces that drove him. Redemption was not achieved quietly but through struggle, by raging against the oncoming storms by being one himself. It was time for the Wraith to make some noise.

'I have one or two ideas,' said Michael with a slight smile.

Loman stood at the centre of the cylindrical Conclave Chamber. High above him, seven platforms were spaced out evenly in a circle. Soft light illuminated the silhouettes of each member of the Covenant Conclave that stood upon them. Apart from voice and sex, their identities were concealed. On the other hand, Loman was fully bathed in the beam of a spotlight that shone down upon him. Only he had access to the chamber and knew its exact location in the sprawling labyrinth that made up the Citadel. However, Felix and Mears were also aware of the Conclave's existence. As the governing council of the Covenant, they were not exactly a secret.

Michael would also learn of them in due course, but Loman had judged it best to ease him into his new world rather than reveal everything immediately. That way, the risk of overwhelming the new recruit was reduced, but, if he turned out to be the wrong choice, then the damage he could do was also minimised. Based on

watching Michael's actions the previous night, Loman
was convinced he had, in fact, made the right choice and
would stand by his recommendation to the Conclave.
Whether or not they would ultimately accept it was
another matter, but as the prior Wraith who had lived
long enough to pass the torch, it was his right to
nominate a successor. Of course, based on recent
history, Loman could understand the Conclave's desire
to tread carefully.

'We watched last night with interest,' began one of
the Conclave members, an older-sounding woman.
'Ryan's abilities are impressive given the limited time
under your tutelage.'

'Thank you, Madam Chair,' responded Loman with a
slight bow of acknowledgement.

'However, that is not to say we have no concerns
about him,' she continued.

'I will concede he is impulsive and passionate,'
admitted Loman. 'Though surely it is encouraging that
what riles him are the very injustices he turned a blind

eye to for so long. It could be said that he is returning to his true nature, his true path even, after taking a wrong turn.'

'Nature? Path?' piped up a male member of the Conclave who stood on the platform to the right of Madam Chair. 'You speak of Ryan as if it was his destiny to become the Wraith.'

'Respectfully, Second Counsel, given his parentage, is that such an outlandish idea? Mistakes made in the past arguably set Ryan on a course that could have been avoided. He is at least owed a chance to realise a better future that could have been his.'

'Let us not dwell on the past, Loman,' pressed Madam Chair. 'That was a different Covenant brought low by its own hubris. Many mistakes were made, and not just concerning Ryan.'

'I am reminded of them every time I look in the mirror,' said Loman bitterly.

'Exactly, and so you all of people know why we must tread carefully,' she continued. 'We simply cannot risk another cataclysm. We barely survived last time. If the Covenant falls, then so too will Dominion City and, eventually, the Imperium itself. Making the wrong choice again could destroy everything we have worked to protect for over a century.'

'Then have faith that choice and destiny have met this time,' advocated Loman. 'I believe that Michael Ryan can be the champion we need. He strayed but has now found his true calling. We are all owed a chance at redemption. Sol knows, I keep working towards mine.'

A third Conclave member, this time standing on a platform behind Loman, spoke up.

'We all saw Ryan's anger issues. He was a hair's breadth away from losing control last night and succumbing to a base desire for vengeance, not justice,' said the sceptical male. 'I agree with Madam Chair that with so much at stake, we cannot risk events turning out like last time. Only the truly righteous should wield the power of the Wraith.'

'Then why was I entrusted with it?' challenged Loman. The previous speaker did not answer. 'Besides, ever since Iron-Wraith first donned his mask, it has always been the way that the Wraith should blend both light and dark,' he continued. 'He knew that most people believe themselves to be righteous in their own minds, that such thinking can lead to the kind of absolutes that almost destroyed us. A good man tainted by some evil has a clearer perspective than most.'

'That was very poetic, Loman, but the fact remains there are still questions involving Ryan, not least whether he is willing to cross the line,' said Madam Chair. 'As Emeritus Wraith, the choice of successor is yours to make, but it is for this Conclave to affirm. Ryan has demonstrated enough promise to warrant a probationary period, but be under no illusion that we will be watching him closely before we give our full assent.'

Loman mulled a moment before conceding that it was the best he would get.

'Thank you, Madam Chair,' he said and bowed slightly.

The lights above each Conclave member shut off, and they disappeared into the darkness, the meeting concluded. Loman slowly walked towards the exit. Probationary periods were not unusual for new Wraiths, so he was not unduly worried. What did concern Loman was the question of whether Michael was capable of crossing the line. He hoped that his instincts were right and that Michael never would. However, if Loman was wrong, there would be no choice but to kill the new Wraith, just as he had been forced to put down the last one.

To be continued in...

ABOUT THE AUTHOR

IJ Benneyworth is a British writer. He spent several years working in the film and television industry, including on *Doctor Who* and *Sherlock*, before becoming a political scientist. He regularly writes novels, novellas, and short stories, including *The Amanda Northstar Mysteries*, the *Queens of the Steal* heist-thrillers, and the *Legends of the Wraiths* series.

Printed in Great Britain
by Amazon

27758699R00165